NORTH
NEW SCOTTISH WRITING

NORTH

New Scottish Writing

EDITED BY JACKIE KAY

The Scotsman & Orange
Short Story Award 2004

First published in Great Britain in 2004 by Polygon
an imprint of Birlinn Ltd, West Newington House,
10 Newington Road, Edinburgh EH9 1QS
www.birlinn.co.uk

Editorial arrangement and Introduction © Jackie Kay, 2004
Contributions © the Contributors, 2004

Typeset in Minion by Hewer Text Ltd, Edinburgh,
and printed and bound in Great Britain by
Creative Print & Design, Ebbwvale, Wales

A CIP record for this book is
available from the British Library

ISBN 1 904598 10 2

The publisher acknowledges subsidy from

Scottish
Arts Council

towards the publication of this volume

CONTENTS

Introduction

JACKIE KAY

'In short stories it is better to say not enough than to say too much, because – because I don't know why!' This was as true for Chekhov in 1888 as it is today. It is beguiling that Chekhov, one of the greatest short story writers of all time, should say 'I don't know why'. It is always fetching when writers are not self-conscious and self-analytical about why they do what they do, because thinking too much about what makes a story work can compromise the story or tie it up in knots.

The world of the short story is still a brave new world; it welcomes pioneers and experimenters and adventurers. There is something that must remain forever enigmatic at the open heart of the short story. It is for this reason that aficionados love it, with such passion. Chekhov thought of story as enigma, and detail – even visual detail – as story, so that not a single word in a Chekhov short story is extraneous. Some readers dislike short stories because they stop too soon or start too late. A short story combines what is wonderful about poetry – language, voice, love of the moment, detail, – with what can be wonderful in a novel – a narrative voice, a way of telling, a different kind of camera lens.

Every word matters in a short story. As Flannery O'Connor, another class-act story writer said: 'A story is a way to say something that can't be said any other way, and it takes every word in the story to say what the meaning is.' A story can live in the moment and take off like a poem; it can soar and end abruptly. But most of all, a short story can truly take you by surprise, shake you up. It should leave you thinking about the moment after the story finishes and the moment before it began. It should leave plenty space for the reader to come in and participate. A short story demands more from the reader than a novel because the reader is told less. If novels sometimes spoonfeed the reader, short stories ask her to feed herself. Some readers love the short story form for this very reason, and for this very reason others dislike it. A short story can truly experiment in the way people often find tiresome in a whole novel. A short story can be completely voice-driven. Every true story should have a voice. The short story is such a perfect form; you should really be able to lift it up and carry it into a huge cornfield, place it bang in the middle and it should still glow.

Maybe the most wonderful thing about the short story is the fact that you can contain an entire story in your head in the way that you can contain a poem, but not an entire novel. You can carry it around with you all day, all week, puzzling over the meaning of it. You can marvel at the way Raymond Carver uses furniture to explore the disintegration of a marriage, the way the objects become events in 'Why Don't You Dance?'. Most of the story happens off the page; we imagine what has happened to the man to get him out in the street selling his furniture. Carver said: 'I love the swift leap of a good story, the excitement that often commences in the first sentence, the sense of beauty and mystery found in the best of them; and the fact – so crucially important to me back at the beginning and even now still a consideration – that the story can be written and read in one sitting. (Like poems!)'

A short story, like a poem, is a small moment of belief. The characters in the best short stories are always snapped at crucial moments in their lives. Something is already shaking them up – grief, divorce, change. Short story writers put their characters through the paces. Here's the wonderful Flannery O'Connor again: 'Being short does not mean being slight. A short story should be long in depth . . .'

Scottish writers from Robert Louis Stevenson on have always loved the short story and experimented with the form. Just think of all the writers today who truly live and breathe in the story form. Think of James Kelman, whose stories to me are even finer than his novels. Ali Smith, whose original and exhilarating stories are truly breathtaking; Michel Faber, whose stories are so varied and fresh as to seem as if they are written by different writers; Janice Galloway; Alan Spence; the totally unique Alasdair Gray; Agnes Owens; the intelligent voice of Shena Mackay; the cool voice of Candia McWilliam, the powerful and profound stories of A L Kennedy.

Here's a collection which shows off the Scottish short story – its lovely capacity for shrewdness, its acuteness, its ability to go straight to the heart, its love of language and voice. There is no story without voice and no voice without story. A story should stay with you like a memory of love long after the lover has left. You should still be able to hear the voice, the song. There are many new voices in this collection of stories and many ways of interpreting our theme of North.

Chekhov once said that when he was writing plays he felt as if somebody was standing behind him looking over his shoulder, uncomfortable, shifty, but that when he was writing short stories he felt free. A writer needs to feel confident in the form itself and the short story is a difficult and challenging form to master. What makes a story really work? Does something need to happen? Does somebody need to change? Is it the voice of the story? Does thinking about what makes one short story a masterpiece and another good and another poor help in the writing of them? Not necessarily. Writing stories is one of those wonderful activities, a bit like sex, the more self-conscious one becomes the less good one is at it.

What is lovely about these stories is their lack of self-consciousness. Here are 20 completely fresh, vivid and different stories from the North about the notion of the North. I hope that sometime soon publishers will push collections of stories with the same amount of dedication and dosh that they push novels. Spring for the short story is in the air. It is the perfect form for our times.

In 'Taking the Flight Path' 'a sliver of moon rises slowly over new land,' which could well be a good description for the short story itself. The language in this story sings, yet nothing much happens, nothing much needs to happen. It is a story of a journey from Scotland to Spain. In many of these stories we get a sense that a new Scotland is emerging; a new, more diverse, more open, more culturally mixed Scotland. Scotland's past and Scotland's future come together in this journey to Spain. It is all in the language here, a rough and heady mix of Scottish images and Mediterranean ones. The window is open wide now in the Scottish short story and that a new confidence is coming out of Scottish writers – a different kind of confidence maybe from the previous generation, one that reflects a changing and emerging country. But Scotland has always produced great story writers and that long courtship with the short story seems set to continue. 'Silk Knickers, Hard Floor', 'All She Had to Do Was Wait', 'Strange Glitter: A Fairytale' and 'Slow Train' illustrate the range and diversity of Scottish writing now. Some stories are written in broad distinctive Scots pioneered by previous generations of poets and novelists – the Kelmans, the Leonards, the Lochheads.

At the beginning of the winning story 'Masonry', a jealous woman scales the wall of a favourite restaurant in New York where her lover sits nonchalantly cheating on her with another woman. It's a heady mix of ideas: jealousy and buildings – how might they connect? Is jealousy the opposite of civilisation? When somebody is madly jealous are they doing something quite unnecessary, but admirable, like climbing Everest? Short stories work in this lovely way; we can puzzle over them for some time after wondering what else the story is about beyond the story that we have on the page. The woman who scales the wall in 'Masonry' keeps us on our toes. I like a tense story. I like the nail-biting anxiety; I like worrying about whether or not she is going to fall. I like to read a short story with my heart in my mouth. From the very first sentence, 'Things seemed to be looking up too,' we are already in that subtle and intense world of the short story. When we come back to that sentence the second time around, the full impact hits us. 'Masonry' explores, as the woman scales the wall, how precise and unrealistic an emotion jealousy is, and how repetitive. It's another fitting image of a new Scotland, of all the dangers involved in trying to claim the past. By the time the jealous woman reaches the top, she realises that the climbing itself is what has defined her and what is really important, not the relationship. 'Masonry' pulls the impudent stunt off because we believe she is doing it. Sometimes the best short stories are those that involve the reader in believing something incredible and believing that other world to be true, to possess a kind of truth that is more blunt and honest than the 'real' one.

'Moving' is a subversive story set in a surreal setting where Edinburgh is Edinburgh and yet not Edinburgh and the people in the story are Scottish and yet not Scottish. This is a high-voltage story that takes you on a rollercoaster ride through the past into the present, by way of the well-known department store Jenners, in the wild and wonderful hands of Royston and Cran, the Time-and-Motion men. The language of this story is gloriously alive and makes the reader jump with the writer from one association to another. 'Cross Words', an enjoyable crime story set in the days before CCTV, also shows off Edinburgh, and words.

Time – fast time, slow time, contained time, time over a number of years, hours, minutes; how a writer deals with the concept of time is the good short story's beating heart. 'Forty Minutes' makes us think about how specific time is, how time can be held in the hand, how it takes minutes to change a life. This is a story about love and it is also a patient study of depression. Angela is having her session with Dr Fraser, her psychiatrist, when she has a revelation.

'White Food, Red Food' uses disjointed lines and fractured language to reflect a split culture, a Chinese past where a baby is buried at sea. The story follow La's – the central character in this singing prose – family's journey from China to the Highlands, where the slow sense of time up there is a source of irritation, mindful of the joke that in the Highlands there is no word that conveys the urgency of *mañana*. 'Such ditherers, these Scottish people.' 'White Food, Red Food' is a lyrical story, that uses language in a poetic way, and is a fresh voice merging the brevity of the haiku with the beef of the folk tale – fresh ginger in a small jar.

Containment, rather than contentment, is a theme that emerges from many of these Scottish stories. People are trapped and contained in their lives, and these stories reflect ordinary people's struggle to be themselves. 'Let It Be' tells the story of a prostitute taking her mind off the job, as it were, by immersing herself in Beatles' songs. There is an appealing redemptive wit in this story. Michelle is trapped in a car, just as the central character in 'Masonry' is clinging to a wall. The short story is such a pure and distilled form that it can brave moments of anguish or shame or anger and stay there. We can take it in a short story; sip it neat like a nippy malt.

'Our Big Day Out' and 'Joy' both explore motherhood or rather lost motherhood in very different ways. 'Our Big Day Out' is a moving and yet unsentimental story, intimate and full of longing.

The short story is a great vehicle for original ideas. Some stories are ideas dressed up in clothes. 'Aurora Borealis' and 'The Weight of the Earth and the Lightness of the Human Heart' both follow the idea to the end of the story. Sometimes the idea itself becomes a character and a plot; Aurora is a lovely girl who bruises easily! Characters in stories are often propelled to change their looks because of their actions. The 'innocent' man in 'From the North' shaves off his entire beard to reveal the stranger's face beneath, 'a pink child's complexion not much changed from the pink child of the winter storm '

What is exciting about these stories is how totally different they are from each other, how each writer has a unique and particular voice. The Scottish voice in 'North of the Law' is unusual and distinctive, the language moody and vivid as bad weather. The very first sentence draws us into its world: 'An' now, rain draps drum oan the panes while the skail pipes up a pibroch in the lum.' How quick the story writer has to be to create the place, the voice, the character. It is a different kind of painting. In 'Seaborne': 'The street's greyharled expressions scar in the winter gales and rain . . . The small house's yard leers over the edge of a balding cliff.'

The short story is like a puzzle that is never ever completely solved. As 'Dr Fenton' says: 'When I was young I wanted to see death, and when I saw it, it seemed to me the ultimate stilling. Its mystery remained with me always.'

Vignatharam in 'Landing in the North' welcomes his passengers aboard his bus. This is a heart-warming and funny story that drives us straight into a new Scotland. 'He is remembering the little bird his aunt kept in a cage at her house back in Sri Lanka. He always adored its fluting song and has sometimes thought of buying a canary to keep as a pet here in Edinburgh for old times' sake.' A singing talking bird! There's as good a definition of the short story as any!

Great writers of the short story have always taken big risks. It is a risky business, full of potential shafts and dangers. You can fall in and not come out again. It is experimental, intense like a brand-new love affair; nobody knows how it will turn out.

Taking the Flight Path

LYDIA ROBB

The fan above the optics chirrs like a cricket, stirring the air to a thick soup. Sweat, alcohol, coconut tanning oil, stale Arpege. Through the wrought iron grid of the window, the walls opposite bounce harsh angles from the mid-day sun. Nothing moves in the white monotony of street. Ruth watches momentarily through the gaps in the curtain then slips back to the kitchen.

Blue-black mussels in the pot. Clack, clack clack, old women's teeth. She draws them from the flame, leaves them steaming under a blanket of tinfoil. She sets two plump Spanish onions on the worktop. Half-moon shapes fly from the blade of her knife, pinwheel across the black marble.

A stem of ash has grown from the Embassy Regal, stuck to her lower lip. The temperature is steadily rising in the pokey kitchen, condensation streaming down the walls between gorgonzola-coloured grout. She checks the thermometer, pours a coffee which she knows she'll never drink, picks an ant from the sugar bowl with the point of the spoon.

> *Summer time an the livin' is easy*
> *Fish are jumpin' an the cotton is high.*

The lyrics well up in her throat, thick and syrupy, then die.

Buenos dias, Ruth. A chirpy voice from behind the beaded curtain.

Och, it's yersel, Cal. Her reply sends ash swirling in a pale flurry into the blackened pan. It amalgamates instantly with the saffron yellow contents. She stirs vigorously. The mixture is at a crucial stage and liable to stick.

As she turns towards the fridge, a movement on the floor stops her in her tracks. A fat, jet-bead of a cockroach lurches towards her foot. She shivers, lifts the sole of her espadrille, waits for the satisfying crunch. The cooking done, she heaves the pan from the stove, discards the few unopened mussels.

Pearls before swine, she thinks. Why bloody bother with paella? Give them what they want. Burgers, mince and potatoes, pie and beans. In echo to her sentiments, Cal's voice comes again. *That mince an tatties I'm smellin?* She doesn't answer. There's a pause. *Five days fae hame an ken whit? I've goat withdrawal symptoms.* Laughter ripples from unseen mouths.

She opens the freezer, takes out a plastic carton, sticks it in the microwave. Sweat spangles her forehead, traces salty lines down her cheeks and into the hollow of her neck. She pushes her damp hair aside with the back of her hand, smells the pungency of garlic from her fingers.

Beyond the fly-speckled window, the sky is an intense Mediterranean blue. A few vibrant nasturtiums cling stubbornly to the cracks in the white stuccoed wall. At the edge of the pantiled roof, two plump pigeons are preening themselves in a display of courtship. A smattering of white feathers drifts languidly earthwards. Snowflakes. She could weep at the absurdity of the thought. Uncorking the coarse red, kept for cooking, she pours herself a generous measure. February. She imagines the weather back home. Cold, with freezing haar spirling up the firth, the grey North Sea stretching to infinity.

A loud *ping* from the microwave interrupts her thoughts. She retrieves the portion of mince then drains the last of her wine. Ewan clatters into the toilet. Some wit has penned a message on the door. *Time Share. Apply within.* There's a clunk as the wooden seat goes down, toilet roll unreeling, the handle flushing. She knows he won't wash his hands. He emerges, zipping up his fly. *Get your arse next door, eh hen?* he says, parting the beaded curtains with nicotine-stained fingers.

Hoi! Are ye no comin ben, doll? shouts Cal. The freckled mirror confronts her with a faded image of herself. She quickly applies some waxy pink lipstick, runs her fingers through her hair and puts on her 'customer' face. She turns the flaring gas jets to a ring of blue pinpricks, slips through to the bar.

The figures on the other side of the counter slowly drift into focus. A group of regulars from Newcastle and a long-faced woman with a gash of scarlet where her mouth should be. Opposite, a man in blue checked shirt, denim shorts and thick woollen socks, his wife in a shapeless dress braided with ric-rac, the daughter shrink-wrapped in pink lycra.

Knowing what's expected of her, she slowly raises her hands above her head, clicking thumb and forefinger together and performs a little flamenco-style dance in time to the guitar music thrumming from the hi-fi. Sweat darkens the patches under her arms like twin maps of Africa. The customers clap. *Bravo. Bravo.* One voice rises above the rest. *Get them aff, darlin!*

Cal is on his feet, a pink carnation tucked behind one ear. Ewan is polishing glasses behind the bar, a thick blue shoelace of a vein ticking at his temple. He screws the dishcloth into a tight ball before directing a fist at Cal. *Shut it, you!* Three syllables with an ominous ring. Ruth looks from one to the other, raises an eyebrow. *He's only kiddin. That right, Cal?* she says, prodding him in the chest. *Naw,* he muttered under his breath, *I wisnae.*

Black curls cling to his head in a crinkled skull cap. He might have been mistaken for a local, with his olive skin and dark eyes. A gold sovereign nestles in the hair escaping like wire wool from the neck of his shirt. Good-looking, in a coarse kind of way, Ruth thinks. She jerks her head towards Ewan. *How to make the Happy Hour unhappy, eh?* Then arms folded over her breast, she laughs her infectious laugh. In no time the conversation has reached its previous raucous level.

The blonde from Newcastle hooks the heels of her snakeskin shoes onto the chromium rung of the bar stool and pulls herself up till she's level with Ewan. She pushes at the bridge of her glasses, her eyes owl-like behind thick lenses. *It's me birthday pet*, she says giving him her order. *Four gins and tonic, love.* She hesitates. *Make them doubles.* Ewan is unimpressed. *Ice and lemon?* he queries dourly in response.

Ruth makes a circle with her hands and lifts the glasses from the bar. The ice in them tinkles bell-like as she moves. *Have one yourself pet*, says the blonde, *seeing it's me birthday*. For the first time, Ruth breaks a self-imposed rule and accepts. *Cheers.* The lemon bubbles trickle over her tongue. By the time she's emptied the glass, her blood pressure is down and the room has taken on a more acceptable appearance.

A brash rectangle of sun lays itself on the yellow ochre tiles at Cal's feet. He looks up, fork poised in mid-air. He gesticulates towards the Se Vende sign. *No really serious*, he says between mouthfuls of food, *aboot sellin up, are ye?* He asks for some HP sauce then proceeds to mash his mince and potatoes into a satisfying brown morass. She would let the place go for nothing, given the chance. *Costa wouldnae be the same withoot YOU.* He pushes the peas and carrots to one side, orders another San Miguel.

At six o'clock Ewan puts up the shutters. Early closing, Monday, his night out with the boys. Boys! Not one of them under fifty. Bingo night at the Ex-pats' Club. Legs eleven. All the fives. Fifty, fucking five.

Ruth slides into the still-hot car seat. On the peninsula a few straggly palms tilt in silhouette against the setting sun. Tomorrow will be another scorcher. Half way to the cash-and-carry she switches on the cassette player. Ewan's tape. Boxcar Willie. Shite. She pushes the eject button and slots in Ravel's 'Bolero, Adagio'. She stops at the beach, lights a cigarette, lets the smoke drift lazily out the window.

Somewhere in the distance she can hear the faint lamentation of an ambulance siren, the thin ululation of a car alarm. A plane is making its descent into Malaga airport, the cabin lights dowsed in preparation for landing. She pictures the expectant faces at the oval windows, straining for a first glimpse of their holiday destination. The doors will open and they'll be decanted into the hot foreign night smells. Parents with fractious children in tow, rushing towards the carousel, waiting for an eternity while everybody's suitcase but their own dances past in an never-ending figure of eight.

Thoughts re-assemble themselves. She points her finger at the night sky, traces the flight-path home. Edinburgh and a one-way ticket to freedom.

Her cigarette is down to a glowing stub. She flicks it from the window then leans over to the glove compartment. She tugs the ring-pull from a can of Schweppes and it opens with a faint sigh. Next she unscrews the cup from the flask, fills it to the brim and taking care not to spill the contents, opens the car door. Feeling slightly disembodied, she walks slowly towards the edge of the promenade.

She cups her chin in her hands, leans over the edge and watches as the dark currents suck and swirl below, the sea inhaling and exhaling the sad, salt scent of tears. Spume rises like fine gauze. Ghosts tugging at the hem of her skirt. Resisting the pull of gravity, she moves away, hands trembling as she drains the dregs from the cup

Oh, your Mama's rich
An your Daddy's good lookin'
So hush little baby, don't you cry . . .

She looks towards the apartment, empty but for the waiting cat. She pictures the cool tiled floor, the expanse of sterile white wall, the blue of the flickering television, beaming its endless British pap.

A sliver of new moon rises slowly above the land. She draws back her arm, throws the empty tin as far as she can into the sea.

Her stiletto heels click like castanets on the terrazzo. She turns briefly, reflecting for a moment. The tin is a receding dot. It too is going the wrong way, reeling drunkenly towards the coast of Morocco.

Masonry

ROB MCCLURE SMITH

Things seemed to be looking up too.

So when I spot him leaving the theatre with her, I'm more than surprised. You see, he told me they didn't even *talk* anymore. So I shadow them, naturally, as they stroll (hand in hand no less) cross-town and into the concourse of the Boaz Regency where – and this I know immediately – they will be lunching in our rooftop restaurant.

My heart is breaking. It's our special place. For birthdays and anniversaries and the most special of special celebrations only. Of course, I'm sure there are explanations, so many explanations, but I don't want to hear them now, or ever.

I meant to surprise him. That's the only reason I was even there in the first place. The photographer had some kind of seizure, an epileptic thing (for one horrible moment we thought he was really dead), and the shoot had to be cancelled for the day. So I wasn't dressed for a meal exactly. Dip-dyed knit shawlkini, stiletto-teeter heels and Miyake A-line panelled white leather mini-skirt aren't your ideal lunch attire. Not quite *prêt-a-manger*. But I thought we could still grab a bite to eat in the park, toss grain at the pigeons by the gazebo, the usual romantic stuff. If the outfit were to attract the occasional gawker, well, we'd cope. We're both used to being looked at.

Now what? I can feel my mascara track in drippy rivulets over the cheekbones that made my portfolio what it is today. I must resemble a startled raccoon. But I also know what I have to do in the circumstances. It's obvious, isn't it?

I palm the surface of the building and look up the sheer face. It's a 400-foot traverse sporting chunks of quartz and rough-cut sandstone set in cement, but lined with thin hand cracks about an inch and a half wide. Perfect. I begin in the north-east corner, behind a convenient scrabble of bushes. First, I take off my watch and earrings and clasp metal bracelet and wrap them inside the ridiculous transparent shawl concoction. Folding the material over, I place it carefully on the thin grass beneath the bushes. Then, looking up, gauging distance, I kick off my heels and jam my hands and toes deep into the declivities.

In no time, I'm hanging off the wall thirty feet off the ground. My legs are shaking and my fingers cramp. A crowd is already gathering on the sidewalk below.

'She's crazy,' screams the homeless guy with the antler cap.

'Ah can see aw the way up yir skirt, hen,' observes the doorman. 'Furst-class view tae. Ye urnae wearin' panties.'

These days, I often meet my compatriots in the strangest places. Given his crassness, I assume this one must be a novelist moonlighting as a doorman.

They both have a point though.

But most people stroll by in the street below in their little ties and coats blissfully oblivious. They only see *city*. Grids of lines negate forever a shot at sublimity. Blinking crosswalks fetter the will to pierce the heart of these quotidian urban mysteries. Walk. Don't walk. Tunnelunkers of the everyday, how will they ever see the light? How do so many of them find the strength to put their clothes on in the morning? And where on earth do they *find* those clothes?

Through the glass, I see a fluorescently lit fan room crisscrossed with massive metal ventilation ducts and humming bright pink, orange and turquoise machinery. A steep stairway of switchbacks ascends out of sight. Clusters of floodlights stud airshafts covered with decades of graffiti scrawl, scribbly-black layers of inscrutable hieroglyphs. Crouching by a fusebox, an electrician in lapis lazuli overalls looks up and drops, sequentially, his gavel and his jaw.

Oh, and what I wouldn't give right this second for a nice bag of chalk and a pair of form-fitting green cuspidal shoes.

The police officer is speaking into a loudhailer, but from these heights he's just a jumble of words and static, a signifying mess.

The larger convention room on this wing is dark and appears empty at first. But now I realise that there is some kind of Shriners' meeting in progress. There are men in fezzes penned by the ghostly triangulation of three burning candles. I hear a muffled chanting. Or am I merely silent witness to a Turkish wedding?

Climbing, the pearl necklace he gave me for my birthday rubs cold as oceans against my bare breasts.

I'm on the main hotel level now, and most of the rooms have curtains drawn. Not this one. On one of the beds a couple make love. She's a big girl, bouncing up and down like a demented hoppy, her eyes screwed shut in concentration. The man is lying on his back behind her, glancing around the room, apparently distracted. I hate that look in men. Then he sees me. There's a partially naked girl in a white leather mini-skirt buildering outside his hotel room window. He smiles and waves. Maybe he thinks I'm a fantasy, a libido-exported hallucination. His lover sees nothing, rhythmically bobbing still, this oscillating tub of merry flesh. I wink at him and keep right on climbing. Men. Honestly.

I still can't believe he's doing this to me. The two of them probably kicked it into gear again when I was on the swimsuit job in the Turk and Caicos. Stupid, stupid. My poor keelhauled heart is a tattered vessel now. He used to crack wise about her thick ankles, smiling like a leopard. But watching his eyes poodle after her Manolo Blahniks on that Milan runway, I knew he still found her only too mattressable.

I'm looking for finger-sized edges and not-too-slopey footholds, finessing my way up, hanging on to some less than encouraging holds. The hotel windows are a slippery slope of glass, but the steel couplings serve as fulcrums. This is not too difficult really. Right angles, horizontals, and perpendiculars mostly. We're hardly talking the Obelisque de la Concorde or the Luxor Pyramid. I raise my left foot up first and then, very carefully, lodge the heel of the right into its hollow to form the angle of a square. The repetition of this motion causes me to rotate slightly clockwise across the face of the building from west to east, but I'm making rapid progress.

On reflection, she must be doing something in the bedroom I haven't heard about, some secret erotic position that's thoroughly gross and distasteful.

On the sixth floor, a window swings open and a police officer's head pops out like a cuckoo from a Swiss clock.

'Young lady,' he says, 'this is way illegal. Not kosher at all. If we don't have you for trespassing, it'll be for indecent exposure. Climb in here this instant.'

'No thanks,' I tell him. 'I'm on a mission here. I'm turning engineering and architecture into a very personal challenge. Also, I'm doing this revenge number on my ex-fiancé. You might go so far as to call it allegorical. So I'll just be heading on north from here. See you at the top.'

'Where ya from?' he says. 'I like your accent.'

'Glasgow. I'm a Scottish model. A fashion model.'

'Land of the shining leather, right?'

'Something like that.' I mean, he's not far wrong.

He looks thoughtful for a second. ''Well, *caution* is the word.'

On the seventh floor, I'm rather surprised to find discarded chalk from some previous climber's foray. Far across the rooftops, reflecting the lake's summer shimmer, I see the dizzying heights of the Tubalcain Towers.

His mother never liked me. That was an issue from the start. I should never in a thousand years have said the thing about her flatulent cat.

Climbing, I don't have time to think about fear or to appreciate its imminence. Fear is a mechanism forcing me to choose the best solution as soon as possible. I feel an intense, almost surrealist, fear-pleasure and, now I'm able to channel the sensation quickly, to master it. I'm doped on adrenaline rush. Me, fearless spiderwoman, daredevil, urban monkey, Xtreme adventurer, cheatee. If you're wondering if it's exciting to be close to falling (because, honestly, by now I have been near to doing so dozens of times), I'd have to say that, at the precise moment of slip, no. Not at all. Afterwards, in the Zen moment of reflective safety, that's a most definite yes. It is as though I were being reborn again and again, every instant a revelation of death's sweet proximity. Did I mention it was a rush?

He called the anniversary dinner I cooked specially for him 'Chicken Fiasco'.

On the ninth floor, I come upon a fellow lying in bed apparently masturbating before his TV. I assume he's engrossed in some bad hotel cable porn until, edging up, I notice that he's watching me, spreadeagled on the facade, as featured on the local cable news. I rap on the window and he looks up, startled. He drops his open right hand to his left side, holding the thumb next to the chest, and lets it fall quickly, glaring at me malevolently all the time. Then he turns back to the screen and picks right up where he left off. That would be just another sign of the times, if you ask me.

Looking down at the mosaic pavement I estimate that the crowd clustered below can now be measured in the hundreds. This must be the best show since 'The Human Fly' climbed the Majestic in downtown Detroit in the '30s in his white tennis shoes and rimless spectacles.

It's on the eleventh floor that I nearly fall. I'm hanging onto the face of the building with one hand, reaching sideways and upwards with the other, when a chunk of concrete snaps off. Frankly, I was hoodwinked by its stolid front. An audible gasp wafts up from below. I pick up the dislodged piece and hand it to Hiram Abif, my agent, who materialises at an adjacent window.

'Thanks,' he says, tossing it inside the hotel room. 'I was seeing you on the telly. You know, after this, your career is lifting-off mode. Whoosh. Into stratospheric. Imagine publicity now. We break America! I tell you, supermodel status is soon. Could Kirsty

Hume be doing this? I think not.' He turns suddenly reflective. 'Just don't fall to horrible squishy death,' he adds.

'Now is not a good time, Hiram,' I tell him. 'By the way, Kirsty is a consummate abseiler.'

The sharp edge of the broken brickwork has pierced my left breast and I'm bleeding. I pull up to the twelfth floor. What are we all really beneath the skin? Skull and bones.

'I have shirt for you,' Hiram yells. 'Stella McCartney,' he adds, sheepishly.

I lean back over the edge and grip his outstretched hand. 'Hiram, this is personal, not promotional.'

'Don't tell me,' he shouts, 'chap lets you down again. What was I saying you often? Models shouldn't date till retirement. Never English men. And not ever actors at all. Engagement is snapping now? Incidentally, Vendela by now would very certainly be wearing shirt.'

No-one could ever accuse my Lebanese agent of having the wisdom of Solomon.

'See you when I see you,' I say.

Not a living soul is eating at the restaurant level. The patrons' open mouths are pressed to the glass in a thick-lipped row. It's the kind of display you pay to see at the aquarium. Their meals have been abandoned. All their sweets *desserted*. I can see small piles of discarded grapes, white napkins scrunched. I am most definitely expected. She gapes my way, wide-eyed, clutching at him. She's wearing last spring's Jasper Conran, a dusky pink Riviera affair with low-waisted trousers and a skinny tie belt. I can't see her shoes, but I can imagine. It's all very sad. Having climbed here to make some unforgettable, dramatic gesture, I now realise that my coming was itself the gesture.

The rooftop has a serious overhang. My legs are quivering. Joyously afraid now, I stretch an arm up for a hold, leaning out over the space, an eternal drop below. My fingers feel for the edge. I have it with my fingertips, now with both hands.

Gripping, I let my feet swing out in a pendulum motion. I'm dangling. I'm falling.

No I'm not. Silly. There's an order to things still. A single pull-up. Left knee down. One leg over, two. I roll onto the roof and lie there on my back, gasping, looking up at the blue ceiling and the one blazing star overhead. I'm laughing hysterically. It feels fine to be so alive in this intense a universe.

'Kiss me hard,' I tell him. He is tall and surprisingly attractive for a Chicago police officer. I have rarely been drawn to men in uniform unless they are portraying men in uniform.

'You're under arrest,' he says, cuffing and most certainly not bussing. He looks me over slowly, a seductive sweep. 'You're something, aren't you? I'll get your number when we book you.'

Overhead, the chopper hovers low and his hair puffs behind his ears in the updraft. He hands me his jacket.

'You should be decent for the photographers,' he says.

'I'm never decent for the photographers,' I tell him. I look down over the parapet. 'If I had a parachute this wouldn't be over, you know.'

'Women don't usually pull stunts like this,' he observes, patting his coif.

'What you don't know about women is a lot, vain-boy,' I say. He looks at me curiously. 'There are no taboos or shibboleths any-more. Glass ceilings offer only a prospect of endless glassy sky. Every day now is some new shattering breakthrough.'

I notice a tiny tuft of hair protruding from his ear. 'A guy like you doesn't know the first thing about exfoliating, does he?'

His nervous smile is marmalade sweet and his cologne not at all unpleasant. As he reaches behind me to adjust the cuffs, his thumb traces the length of my fingers, rubbing gently against my knuckle joints. It's then I realise just how far I've come.

Moving

JOHN ABERDEIN

– And a Merry Christmas to you too, sir. When it comes.

Heading for the exit they stepped off the tartan rug, then waded through blue carpet, a sponge of blue. The tall one reached the revolving door. Lofting his crocodile briefcase, he pressed on the polished flange of brass. The door began to revolve. The stockier, jigging in sideways late, got his heel clipped, *Fu—!*, and the whole jing-bang juddered.

Out on the steps of the North British Hotel they came, out onto North Bridge, where a queue of black cabs purred and waited. He chose to walk. But bare a step when the on-ding came, down came the undammed rain.

– Jumping Jehosophat!

– Bugger it!

– And lil black fishes.

Royston and Cran were the Time-and-Motion men.

Rain to dodge and time to kill before the north train, they approached a Goth of a monument.

– Like devils' cake, said the tall one.

– Do whit? said Cran.

– This freaked-up pile, said Royston. Like devils' cake, black.

– Come again?

– Baked and burnt for that deluded Limey. Stuck in his half-buried tent, storm like a thousand wolves, raving for hot grub, anything, pemmican.

– Ptarmigan?

– Till he froze.

– Wha froze?

– Scott.

– Wha bluidy Scott?

– Then the black gangrene. When they hauled off his gloves his fingers fell out.

– Pull the ither ane.

– His huskies ate them—

– His huskies ate bollocks. Scott was a writer. *Wri-ter*, said Cran.

– That low on fingers? Tough call.

– Listen a minute, it's nae nothin tae dae wi explorin. Scott, see, Scott Monument. Novels—

– Novels? In the name of the big monkey, you get a monument for that? Novels?

– Dinna look at me like that, I dinna read them, Mr Royston. Life's too short, eh?

Royston looked up at the sooty curlicues.

– They had piles o them in Thin's thonder when I was in buyin exercise paper, Cran said. Whit dae they cry them? *Wave, Wave-somethin, The Wavery Novels.*

They entered and paid. Then they began climbing, Cran fitting slip-on shoes to pre-worn grooves in the steps, and saying the syllables, a mindless pacer, as the stairway narrowed.

Sir Wal Sir Wal
Sir Wal-ter Scott
Sir Wal Sir
Wal
ter
Scott
wee pause
reprise

Rain was breaking over Edinburgh in waves from the north-west, darkening the freestone buildings, gusting and spitting from gargoyles as they climbed. Royston and Cran wound up the last tight awkward stair. There was somebody up on the platform, some young man, back to the pillaring, bowed by the elements. He had his book out – *Suicide.*

– Aye, aye. Grand book ye have there, said Cran.

He glanced up.

– Manual? said Royston.

He shook his head.

– Novel? said Cran.

Shake.

– Socifuckinology, said the student.

Then they looked down on Princes Street, where they'd just finished giving Jenners its T&M, its Time-and-Motion, as per commission.

Big store, down on its uppers. *Crème de la crème,* very genteel. They'd arrived and caught them for the Christmas rush.

– Rush? said Royston. Say again? Did I hear you correctly – *rush*?

– Ye see it, said Cran.

– Makes the Erie Canal look like Niagara. Geezers here wouldn't know throughput if it jumped up and bit them in the ass.

– Mebbe no.

So they applied stopwatch-and-clipboard to all the sales staff in turn.

– You wouldn't believe it in a book, said Royston to the manager, in front of his owner. Average time to accost a client and turn one sale?

– Accost? We like to think we make each customer welcome.

– How long are they welcome?

– Ten minutes, perhaps.

– Double that, twenty.

– Well, but surely—

– Your top guy for sure is Mr Sillar. Tugging at wooden drawers, writing out receipts in backhand longhand with a fountain pen for

Chrissake, folding and refolding and patting farewell to each item of garmenting on his glass counter, hiding the goods in oodles of tissue and brown paper and a mile of sisal, he chats to every goddamn client about pesky ministers, best boarding schools, Morgans, scandal, rugby.

– *Morgans?* said the manager. Surely not, that would be in Dundee.

– Wee sports car, said Cran, wi the wire wheels.

Royston spread on the manager's table a three-month acceleration set of service interaction targets: 11 minutes, 8 minutes, 4. The manager murmured *Not that kind of shop.* But the owner said it had better be, Jenners, the chainstores were spreading, *sharp and jewish,* new ones starting up.

– It's *piskie,* Cran'd said, afterwards. *Piskie* ministers. Some in Edinburgh, they worship bishops.

– Believe it.

– The others hae nae time for that. They get on fine. They worship themsels.

Cran rolled his eyeballs down the Gardens, hopped them across the railway lines, and up at the famous Castle with its crusted apron of rock. He nudged at Royston and pointed.

– Wait till one, there's a gun. Cannon.

– Where?

– The Castle, whaur else?

– When?

– One.

– A joy. Who do they shoot?

Cran snorted.

– It's for aa ye invaders. Wait ye here, ye'll get a hole whaur your dinner should be.

– Ouch to lunch indeed, Mr Cran.

– Ye'll be lucky if it's jist your belly they blaw awa.

– Yanks don't invade.

– Eh?

– We just take over.

Cran shared a grimace with the student, as Royston spun. Tracking him on the staircase spiral, Cran jigged and concertinad his thin-suited knees all the way down.

Their fawn shoulders got wet in no time as the wind shoved them back along Princes Street and down the brae, the steep ramp, into Waverley Station.

– Better wi ma bluidy auld trench coat, said Cran.

– Drench coat?

– Trench coat, I says.

– Sure. They explained you served in the weekend army.

– Nae totally weakened. Terriers, eh! We used tae train on Rannoch Moor.

Royston dug out his coins and inspected them.

– Used tae ram oor bayonets in hingin dummies, till the flock burst oot. No for a *Scotsman*?

Royston proffered a silver florin for a copy of the *Financial Times*, pink and thick, plus a pack of strong smokes, Capstan Full Strength.

– Dummies?

He got brown cents back.

– Flock?

Royston looked up at the green glass eaves of Waverley Station. Sources pushed humphs of steam into the air, dank chugs of smoke, and long indicative whistles.

Cran tiptoed, jumped, to scan over the throng.

– Aye, dummies. That's us ower there, Platform 19.

– Rule 1, said Royston. Always stick with a native.

*   *   *

Off the Aberdeen train the carriage doors were hanging, on their strop. They checked that the North British porter had lodged their cases with the guard. They walked along the concrete platform till they came to First Class. Royston led aboard and began sidling along the corridor. He came to a blockage: some skinny guy in a jerkin, a blonde dame neat in uniform. The guy had her double-bolted against the panelling, his bony paws on either side pressed flat.

    – Come on, Billy, get aff.

    – Pardon please, could you budge over?

    – But Ah thocht Ah wis hame wi ye tae Fife.

    – Pardon please.

    – Naw, Billy. Ye're comin tae nae Fife.

    – An inch, fellas?

    – Aw, Dinah!

    – Write tae me ower Christmas, okay?

    – But Ah didna ken whit tae dae.

    – Ye're still the guid man.

    – Do travellers—

    – Rubbish man, ye mean.

    – Retain rights in this country?

    – Ah luve ye, Dinah. Ye ken Ah luve ye.

    – Naw, Billy. Naw.

Billy shut both eyes and pursed his lips. He kept his groin well back, short of touching her.

    – Comin thru!

Billy shot forward, their hips butted, twice, he coughed on her nose.

    – Christ, Billy, really! We're through wi fumblin aboot.

Bundled in his arms, she glanced down the corridor one way and, more awkward, the other. There was no help, there never could be.

Royston slid a compartment door open, and Cran reslid it shut. Ample. They had a six-seater all to themselves. Cran shook out his fawn overcoat, folding the shoulders inwards, then lengthways in two, and nestled it high on the chrome hammock. Royston placed his crocodile briefcase on the spare seat beside him. He had elected the carriage's external window, gazing forward, so Cran sat on the corridor side, looking backward, on the scarlet plush.

Fancy antimacassars had been fastened over the headrests, against greasy hair and falls of dandruff, crocheted *BR. British Railways. Brylcreem.* Cran pressed his head back, nice and quiet on the train. He peeked at the tableau out in the corridor: that skeleton jailing his hot nurse. A special softness under uniform—

The whistle blew, there was a last decisive slam.

The Aberdeen train jerked like a snake immediately weary, that slowed through Princes Street Gardens, a shallow Glencoe, and moulded painfully into the dark bowels of Edinburgh, its six mottled 20-watt bulbs pitiful in their fittings. A fart of eggs rose through their compartment as they ghosted past a criss-cross-criss of headtorches. Some workers, amongst the fallen faeces and the rats, bent about their business, restoring loosened brick.

– See there, Mr Royston, oot there in the tunnel?

– I can hardly look anywhere else.

– There's a bodge-job needin a wee study.

– Whole two-bit country needs one, Mr Cran.

Then they were lost in a gust of smoke.

Stolid faces slid into view, scores of parcels under arms, wrapped in tan or coloured paper, sellotaped and squared with string. Naturally the platform was packed, it was Christmas Eve.

The tableau broke. Cran didn't see the final farewells, for he pulled his corridor blinds down smartish to deter boarders, and harkened the Haymarket shoppers as they shuffled on past. It worked, near on. But then shoes clipped to a stop in the corridor. As the heavy door slid back, there stood the young and fair-haired nurse.

– First Class obtains here, said Royston.

One sideways stride took her round Cran's lumpen knees and patent feet. She arrowed an arm into her dark green duffel-bag, and fished out a book for the journey.

– Obtains whit, whit does it obtain?

– Lady, are you First Class?

Her calves tautened as she flipped the duffel high in the luggage net, then thought she'd need help later, else stand on the seat, she'd made a mistake. She unbuttoned the neck of her black coat, and made to unbutton, but didn't unbutton, the breast. Plunking herself down on the broad window seat, two away from Bulky Boots, and opposite Mister Pushy, she hooked one lock of hair behind an ear, and lowered her eyes into her orange novel, *The Cruel Sea* by Nicholas Monsarrat. She'd no be moving, no for any Yank.

Then she looked up.

– Aye, I'm first class, thanks, fine. How are ye, yersel?

Royston had unfolded the pink acre of his *Financial Times*. He poked his head round and spoke, away from the girl, towards his junior.

– You Brits sure do choose some damn funny colours for newspapers. Dunno what Senator McCarthy is gonna say.

Cran shrugged.

– I'm serious, partner. Nodding towards the nurse. This pinko tendency could spread.

Scabby outskirts, South Gyle, rolling country, Dalmeny next. Good to get away from the capital, her training done. She thought of Billy at Haymarket, tears in a man.

– Smoke, ma'am?

She lost it before she could rerun the unsatisfactory dream.

– Capstan?

It was Mister Pushy, trying to suck in, trying another tack.

– Ta. I dinna bother wi these.

– Really? Guess in your line of country you'd be glad of a puff, now and again.

She thought, No a puff like you.

– Why in ma line o country, would ye think? said Dinah.

– Worry and fret, worry and fret.

– Ye winna catch me frettin, less matron gets up ma back.

– Got to keep the fillies on the pace.

– Oh. Ken aa aboot it, dae ye? Ken aboot hospitals here, then?

– It's Ern actually. Big Ern they call me, said Royston. And you?

– Dinah, if ye must.

– Charmed.

– Dinah, mind. Dinna caw me Diana. Dae ye ken hospitals here, I'm askin?

– If you insist, I ken, know, Chicago.

– Never mind Chicagos. Ye should try our isolation ward.

– With you? A delight.

– No muckle delight. Kids greetin an bawlin the hale nicht.

– Who do they greet?

– Means bluidy cryin, said Cran, looking up from his travel guide of East Coast Scotland.

– O, tears after bedtime. Sure, we all got our little troubles.

Royston lit a fag with his silver lighter. Dinah put her head down to her book, then asked out straight.

– Chicago. Is that whaur Al Capone?

– Yeah. All kindsa slaughterhouse, canneries, the biggest.

– Whit dae ye dae for a livin then, mister, can hot air?

He put his head back as though to smile, and blew a ragged ring. They were drawing out of the small halt at Dalmeny, past some prickly hawthorns, out between the diamonds of the great red bridge.

– Time-and-Motion, to tell you the truth.

– Nivver heard cheep o them afore.

– Taylor's the operator. Taylor International. You will be aware of us?

– Me, naw, I hardly think so. Sae what does Mr Taylor hire guys like ye for?

Cran looked up from the gazetteer he was hiding his face in.

– Upgrading efficiency.

When it came to the Forth, they'd learned their lesson, the guidebook assured, about jerry-building. 5,000 men it took in all, working in shifts for 7 years. They planted and clenched 6,500,000 white-hot rivets. For cladding they daubed on 60 tons of dull red paint.

57 of them died also.

Fell mostly, Cran imagined. Struck on the skull. Or crushed.

Clicketty-CLACK, clacketty-CLICK. Royston put aside his paper. The noise echoed inside the bridge, inside his head, his seat vibrated. Through the window smear, the lattice of railings, through the great angular tubes, he glimpsed downwards. The choppy waters of the Firth of Forth narrowed as he glanced up west, scuds of rain hiding whatever was back there. But looking ahead, through the flicker of each red pillar, he got cubist impressions of a vessel, or vessels. The superstructure of a Navy high in dry dock, turrets in steps, the long grey guns. Clacketty-CLICK, clicketty-CLACK, Clacketty-CLICK, clicketty-CLACK.

RICK-RIICK-RIIICK—

Royston pitched forward, his right palm whanging the dame's forearm, as the train thrust down on hard-braked bogies. Her novel flew.

– For ony pity's sake, said Cran. Some clown's pulled the cord!

But Dinah was past him, first in the corridor.

A carriage door lay banged open. She ran along and clambered down and out onto the wet ridge of ballast. Along the way stood the engine, *shoosh-shoosh, shoosh-shoosh*, pistons arrested, a bull in a pen. But her eyes were for Billy, scissoring over the railings, ant in a huge red web.

   – Billy!

Rain washed in scuds behind him. Billy's left knee buckled, he grabbed some bracket at the very edge. Out in his summer jerkin, he clapped its gappy zip together, and felt its collar flipper at his neck.

   – Naw. Naw, Billy!

Then the squall passed like a hurled veil. Billy stood on the last girder. He looked down at the broad-faced Forth and its poxed Inches, studded irregular with concrete and gulls. Could hear her, worried now, *tap-tap* on the boards towards him.

   The Rubbish Man, trembling a bittie.

   – Easy, Billy.

Like at the Public Baths, high on the springboard once. The attendant below would yell at first-timers *Lowp weil oot!*

   – Steady, Billy. Come on tae Fife.

   On a springboard if you overpinged – back coming down, you'd whack on the jut.

   – Nae problem, Billy. Honest.

   Dinah said after, that he half-turned.

   – BILLY!

   Scenery came for him in a bright, black rush.

*   *   *

Dinah inched her heart to the edge, and gazed over. Three gulls, loosed arrows, were fanning away off the surface. They looked not white, opal.

   It was long past the splash.

When they arrived, the plain clothes, they took her out of the hubbub up to the guard's van.

Rank smell, as they drew her over to a wicker trunk.

– Take the weight off your legs.

A threshing arose from inside, within.

– Easy, lass. Homers.

Then the guard laid his head outside, peering upline, till his eyeballs stung with wind and cinders.

Dinah sat in the cramped toilet a long time. At one point the door started to open, and she leapt up, shoving it shut. She moved the snib. Outside it would now read *Engaged*.

Hunched over her knickers, over her knees, she swore at her gripped shins. *Ye swear like a nurse,* he'd said to her once.

The lid rose with her a little. She leaned on a tap, and read the bossy wee plaques.

Ne pas pour boire. Kein Trinkwasser.

A buff curdle of egg and Flakes whacked round the bowl.

– Got any gum, mister?

– Be my guest.

– Ta. Thanks.

Cran stooped, and picked the orange paperback up by its wings.

– We thought you scheduled to descend at Fife, said Royston.

– Descend? said Dinah.

Chewing slow, she closed her eyes and dozed.

Law agents were gassing with his sidekick somewhere. She had a speck of something on her coat, on the dark button of her gaberdine. He inhaled, paused, then picked a shred of gold from off his tongue.

He blew a lasso.

The train huffed north, through red clawed furrows, blown sketches of coast, at length across a whorled river. A grey stone set slid by, the puffs grew slower.

Royston peered at the board and mouthed.

– *Joint Station*, yeah. *Joint Station*, that about says it.

– Says what? said Dinah, pretending to wake up.

A pigeon swooped then hightailed – up through girders.

– Here already?

One shoe levering on the plush, she hoicked her duffel-bag clear, then stepped back down. She tugged an alloy comb through.

– Bye, Mister Ern.

– Ern Royston.

– Ta for the gum.

– I sure do hope—

But she was off down the corridor.

Forty Minutes

EVELYN WEIR

There is something about the cream blandness of my psychiatrist's office that always makes me calm from the moment I go in. Maybe if I moved in here it would all stop. I think it is the lack of anything to look at; no plants, no pictures, no books, no people, no pain, just three institutional chairs which by now are as familiar to me as my own. There is the wooden one that I wait on, the blue one that I sit on, and one for him which is grey and fuzzy. Nothing else but the blank rough walls and a well-worn desk. And him, of course. I can see small sparkles of sweat on his top lip as he says hello. It is hot, but I keep my coat on. It might not take long today.

'So,' he says, 'how have things been since the last time we met?'

Always a tough one, this. I hate to disappoint him. I always wish I could say 'Well, you know, Dr Fraser, I think I'm better, you've fixed me, so thanks for everything', but really things are just the same, or perhaps a little worse.

'Just the same,' I say, and immediately wonder if I should have lied. If everyone he sees today says 'Just the same' he might go home feeling as bad as I do. 'Just the same,' he echoes, but it is not a question. 'Just the same,' I say again. Well, we've established that, anyway. I feel just the same. Just the same as I have for the last eight months.

Taking a stolen look at him, I think again how nice his hands are. A bit of a waste, him being a head doctor, he should be using those hands to suture expertly crafted essential surgery. Probably thirty-five, he looks older in his doctor clothes, but sometimes when he gets to the painful parts and I need a distraction I imagine him on the side of a mountain with a strong wind disturbing his doctor hair.

'How are you finding the medication?' he asks.

The medication. On it I feel detached from life, I am numb, I have diarrhoea, I sweat, my head is fuzzy, I feel sick all the time, and I still feel bloody miserable.

'Fine,' I say.

'Good,' he says, 'and what about the sleeping?'

I can sort of remember what it was like to sleep through the night, but I can also remember how much I took it for granted. I simply expected that life owed me at least nine hours' unbroken repair, and so it happened that way for thirty years. I went to bed, I slept. Now at thirty-one, at best I hope for one or two hours of fragmented escapist nightmares, and then stay awake reliving the reality for the rest of the night. Sometimes I look out of my window in the black hours and hate the people in the dark houses, because I know they are asleep. If hell on earth exists, it is defined by insomnia.

'Not so good,' I say. As I have fed him a few false positives already, I figure he can handle a negative truth. We talk about sleep a lot when I come here. We discuss ways to feel sleepy a lot. We increase the dose a lot. We increase the dose again a lot. We switch medication a lot. I still don't sleep a lot.

'Oh,' he says, 'because last time you said it had improved.' My mother always said that the trouble with lies was that you have to have a good memory.

There is a pause.

'I can see a bit of general improvement in you, Angela,' he says. We move into the motivational phase. This is the pattern. 'What you have to think about is how far you have come since it happened. You will get better.' When he tells me this I believe it for that moment. 'Recovery is never a straight path, sometimes things will get better, sometimes they may get worse for a short while, but the overall result is better. Think about it as a journey in a car. Try this. Imagine you were going somewhere, maybe to your favourite place.'

I imagine.

'Where are you going, Angela? Where is your favourite place?'
Oh no.

I hate this. Some of the doctors in the beginning just after it all happened would ask about favourites, like favourite colour, or animal or something, and then try to analyse it, like it all fell apart because I like blue and squirrels.

'Up North,' I say.

'Up North?' he repeats. 'Where up North?' Oh no.

'Cape Wrath,' I say.

'Why there?' he smiles.

Because it is beautiful; because the colours of Scotland swirl onto darkened cliffs in a boiling green sea; because it is the last place I felt happy at; because my conscience was sedated; because Callum was there; because in the driving rain we shared a red crunchy apple and some hotel biscuits and waited for the boatman to come back, and it was then, standing looking at the seaweed spilling onto the rain-soaked sand that I knew I loved him. At the top of the cliffs I had noticed a pale rock with strips of pink and grey, and he carried it for miles just because I liked it. I still have it now. Sometimes I think I can smell him on it.

'I don't know, I just liked it there. I'd like to go back.' I smile. He smiles. He is pleased, because I have said something positive, like I'd like to go back somewhere rather than I'd like to die.

'Okay,' he says, '. . . think back to the journey you made to get there.' I think. 'Now,' he says, 'the general direction you needed to go was north. Visualise a compass and a road map. You wanted to get to Cape Wrath, like you want to get better. But you couldn't just go straight; sometimes you might have gone east, west; sometimes you might even have gone south on some roads, round roundabouts; you might even have stopped somewhere and made no progress for a while.'

'Inverness,' I say helpfully, not sure if he was really asking.

'Right!' he says, enthusiastically embracing his analogy, with his top lip sparkling furiously now. It really is incredibly hot. Maybe they think all mad people are cold and turn the heat up. 'Do you see what I mean? Maybe you are nearly at Inverness now. Try not to focus on where you are. Focus on where you have been, how far you have come, and where you are going.' I like this. I like to think that in the map of getting back to being normal I am at Inverness, although I suspect I am in recovery where I am now in reality, somewhere on the outskirts of Edinburgh.

'Let's talk again about your medication. We've only scratched the surface as far as the sleeping drugs go. There are lot more to choose from.' Scratched. Recently I've scratched my own surface quite deeply on regular occasions with a kitchen knife and a little pair of scissors. He isn't worried about that, he says cutting is a 'common transitional stage' and that it will stop. We don't even talk about it any more.

'Okay,' I say. I would swallow the desk his beautiful hands are resting on in small jagged pieces if I thought it would make me unaware of the long hours between two and seven.

I tell him my story yet again. I wasn't always like this, I want him to know. I need him to know I wasn't always this bad. I had the normal things and a normal life. I had intact mental health. In six months my life was gone. A cascade of disaster, reminding us how fragile it all is; that today the sun can be bright, tomorrow the sun may not rise. My mother died on Christmas Day last year. Like the drama queen she was, she had a heart attack just as the turkey was coming out of the oven. Heartbroken, my father followed her four weeks later. No brothers, no sisters, orphaned and alone at thirty-one. I took three weeks off and my contract was not renewed. No job. Filled with grief and after many years of pain I left my husband on a whim, taking two bags of clothes which were getting too big for me by the day, and the really good cheese grater. I liked cheese. He kept everything else. No marriage, then. No stuff.

And now we get to the problem. I left my daughter there that day with her father. As they say in grim voiceovers, 'It was a decision she was later to regret'. My lawyer is very sorry but she can't fix it now. I left, so it is my fault. When I go to her office she looks at me with sympathy, while her children (who are still with her) stare accusingly at me from the photograph frame on her desk. My friends judged me more than my enemies. I hadn't expected that.

Take stock, Angela. No parents. No husband. No child. No friends. No house. No money. No stuff. No self-respect. No future. One cheese grater. No cheese. Breakdown. No mental health. No more. No more, I thought, and swallowed down the means to an end. That was the day it all began. Ambulances, blurs of faces, food in tubes, drug-induced blissful hot sleep and delicious dreams for many weeks. A series of questions. 'Next of kin?' one of them asked me. Hot tears sliding. 'You must have a next of kin.' It would appear not.

And then I met Callum. Having scraped together enough to rent a place to lie between hospital admissions, I was out in the real world, buying cheese, as it happens. A tall broad man was behind me. I looked at him and he looked back at me, and I saw something. Despite the bright lights in the deli illuminating the pain and the dark circles on my pale, thin face, he saw something too. It was Roquefort, it was in my hands, and he said it was his favourite. In a moment of boldness I gave him what used to be my best smile and asked him to come round and share it with me. A stranger in a cheese shop. He gave me his telephone number. I called him when I got home, he came round within the hour, and we ate the cheese. I told him about my pain, and he told me about his. We went to bed together as we both knew we would, in my little rented bedsit in my little rented bed. We curled up naked in each other's anonymity, talked, slept, ate more cheese and stayed there for three days. No sex at that time, because we both knew that would have spoiled it all. They were without a doubt the three best days of my life, and by the end he knew me better than I knew myself.

It was of course a 'bad time' to meet. It was a rocky start, and a rocky course. He held me when I cried, when I raged my fists against his chest and screamed. He took the glass from my hand when I thought the answers lay in oblivion. He held me even when I lay awake rubbing the corner of the blanket in the bleakest quiet moments of self-hatred. I gave him nothing, and took so much. He gave me hope, comfort, assurance and a reason to be. He let me talk about the grief, about the loss, about the pain of missing my daughter. 'Everything will be okay' he would whisper into my hair, like a mantra. 'Everything will be okay'. He came with me to the lawyer, became my voice when the tears spilled. When my daughter came to stay he played guitar while she sang. He fixed me up with bereavement sessions, and came with me to Dr Fraser. He wasn't just my support, he became part of me. I remember thinking one day that perhaps he wasn't real, that maybe there was such a thing as a guardian angel. I thought it so seriously that I got him to walk beside me past a mirror one day, just to see if he had a reflection.

One early morning as we lay in bed with the winter sun screaming us awake through my shabby curtains, he asked me where I would like to go – anywhere at all he said, and he would take me there. He said I needed a break from the little room. He said I had been through so much. I didn't know, couldn't think of anywhere. Then he said he had always wanted to go to up north, to the very top of Scotland. We travelled up through the bleakest weather, browns and greens giving way to greys and deepest black. He drove all the way with one hand, and held my hand with the other. Stunning colours and shapes, sweet promise of hope and happiness quietened me. I would have stayed there forever. We saw Cape Wrath on the map, and knew we had to go. We liked the 'wrath' part, and it didn't let us down. Hard rain and thunder-storms, roaring seas and hypnotising cliffs, the remoteness of it was exhilarating and renewing.

A few weeks after Cape Wrath I woke up one Sunday morning and watched Callum on my pillow. His eyes were closed, his big comforting strongness rising and falling with every gentle breath. He always hugged himself when he slept, and his long arms that offered me such solace were wrapped around his beautiful body. The delicious warm smell he always had was on my sheets and on my face. His smell was hard to define, somewhere between sun-warmed wood and melted toffee, and I loved to fall asleep with my nose pressed hard against his back, taking it in. I was happy. Happy. An incredible rush of panic filled me as I was shocked by the sudden realisation that I needed him. He had to go.

I woke him up, pushed his back hard, and told him to leave. He was sleepily confused, couldn't understand what was going on. He tried to hold me. I told him to go, to get out of my life. I looked into his eyes and told him to leave. 'I don't understand' he had said. He cried. Real tears, real sobs, and I felt nothing but relief. Eventually he left. He called. I didn't answer. He called round. He wrote. He told me he loved me. I knew that, but he killed the pain and I had become used to that. That was why he had to go.

Dr Fraser looks at the floor, then to me. 'Why do you think you did that?'

Because I felt guilty to feel happy, because I want my life to be over, or to be starting, or to be someone else. Because I felt like I was building up a debt I would never be able to repay. Because I was scared.

'I don't know.'

'How do you feel about Callum now, Angela?' he asks.

'I miss him.'

'Do you feel able to get in touch with him? Would you want to do that? How do you think he is feeling?' Three questions.

'I don't know. Maybe. I think he is sad.'

'Sometimes when someone loses a lot, they become afraid when things begin to get better. They worry about the next thing to happen. It is almost as if there is an expectation that things will go wrong, so they may destroy anything positive which comes along –

well, maybe destroy is too strong a word. But they will be afraid. That is normal.'

I nod. Destroy is not too strong a word. He looks into my eyes and I look back into his. He doesn't look into my eyes very much. I guess they told him in medical school to avoid it. Too risky. He is looking now, and it all makes sense.

I know now, more than I have ever known anything else before, that out of great hopelessness can come something else, and that maybe I can give as well as take, build as well as destroy. I feel better. I know that I am heading for Inverness, and I know what I have to do.

The forty minutes are up. He is reaching for his diary to make the next appointment. That is his signal that it is over. It has been really helpful today. Something has happened.

I leave and walk out from the heat into the crisp coldness of the late morning. I take out my phone and hope this will work. I call; it rings. I haven't heard his voice or felt his love for eight weeks and two days. He answers. He asks me how I am, and I say I am getting there.

White Food, Red Food

GERALDINE PERRIAM

Set the table.

White cloth, white bowls, white china spoons, white napkins.

Chopsticks, black lacquer.

Three dishes, china, oxblood glaze, centred.

Green spring onions, chopped, two drops of sesame oil in the white bowls.

They wait for the steaming broth and the silky dumplings.

She waits.

What will he bring?

She waits, as La has taught her.

'Have it all ready and wait. No bustle at the last minute.'

White food, red food. White food first. La's instructions. La's accent like the broth and dumplings: silky, warm. Underneath, pungent.

No rice. Another time, perhaps. Tonight there are mandarin pancakes and shredded chicken. La's dish.

He will expect a banquet. Many dishes at once, spicy, rich. But hers is also La's way. Northern dishes served in the Highlands the way La did for fifty years.

White food, red food. Wait.

La waited. Waited in Shanghai with her first-born. La waited and hated.

When the streets were full of blood and broken glass, the waiting stopped. Second wife and her child lay in the street, cut and bruised.

'Like camellia petals. Wang was dead. I didn't hate the Japanese as much as others. They killed Wang. Horrible man.'

Lying in the muck, the blood, La shielded her child from the soldier's bayonets, hiding behind a packing box near the go-down.

'I lost consciousness and when I woke, I thought I was dead because he was white, this man. A white face looking at me. But it was a foreign devil. That's what we called them. And he looked, just looked. Said nothing for so long.'

'Give me the child,' the man had said and La had screamed.

'The child is hurt,' said the man.

'He spoke to me in my own language. Funny accent but fluent.'

The man, her own grandfather, had lifted mother and child and carried them into the remains of the go-down. The child was dead.

'He wrapped my son in a blanket and put him into the harbour. He used stones to make him sink. He told me. I didn't see. Too busy dying of the fever. He told me later. He couldn't bury him and he couldn't burn him, so he put him into the water.'

'A burial at sea' her grandfather had called it and La didn't understand at all. She was dying of the fever.

Grandfather had bathed her three times a day in a small wooden barrel, quietly soaping her burning body and returning her to the dark corner where she would lie under a quilt. She called to her son and Grandfather would tell her he was safe.

'Safe under the water. I didn't know until the fever went.'

When the fever went, the guns were louder and more persistent. Grandfather took her to the harbour where her son was buried. They took a boat north.

'I saw him properly, then, this white man, your grandfather. Quiet, no fuss. I liked that. He never asked one question except if I wanted to go north with him. He fed only white food to me all the time. I thought it was his treatment for fever but he couldn't find any red food.'

She waits, remembering La's voice, ready to burst with laughter.

La has told her to look first thing when the guest comes. What does he bring and how does he give it?

'If he brings wine, it should be white, not red. No wine is better but they don't bring beer. Beer is good but they think it makes them peasants,' says La, forgetting that her granddaughter is fractionally one of 'them'.

'If they look embarrassed with the wine, it means they know it's wrong. If they don't then they haven't thought at all. But wine is better than chocolates! Chocolate for a dinner from Shantung! Better to bring nothing than chocolate.'

La never liked chocolate and would feed it to the dogs. She would not allow her daughter to give it to the grandchildren.

'Bad food. Give them fruit.'

La's daughter would nod and feed the children chocolate in secret.

La. Called La because she sang to them as children. They would wave their tiny starfish hands at her and say 'La', asking for her to sing. She became La to everyone then.

'Not too much sesame oil. Two drops. That's enough. We northerners like our food delicate, refined.'

As a child, she had tried to emulate La's accent and failed. La spoke with a soft Highland accent; cultivated, seasoned, drawn from the cadence and rhythm of her husband's speech. Now buried, now overlaid, were the clipped tones of the girl from Shantung. No nonsense. La hated delay.

'Such ditherers, these Scottish people. I don't unnerstand.' La, who understood so much could never say the word properly in English.

'I don't unnerstand. They are so practical. No fuss. Oh but they dither. In a Shanghai market they'd be trampled underfoot, squashed. Your grandfather never dithered. He learned in Shanghai: don't dither. That's how we got out alive. He learned in the market and it saved our lives.'

La had followed him without question, knowing that there was no future for her in Shanghai, where her first-born lay at the bottom of the harbour.

'He knew what he was doing. I knew I had lost a child. I thought that maybe there was a chance if I went north. No chance in Shanghai with the Kuomintang.'

She heard the story of La's journey north many times; of her grandfather feeding La, coaxing her back to life.

'What I couldn't unnerstand was why he didn't ask me to marry him or to be his concubine. That's what I was used to. For all he knew I could have been a prostitute or a sing-song girl. I was sold to Wang as his second wife. All my sisters were sold to some man or other. I thought maybe your grandfather would sell me. If I was his concubine, maybe I wouldn't be worth as much.'

He did not sell her. He fed her and kept her warm; kept her from the sailors and their sidelong glances.

'By the time we got to Hong Kong, I couldn't imagine he would leave me but he did. He took me to the nuns and told them what had happened. Then he gave me some money and left. He said he would come back but I didn't think he would. He was like those missionaries who used to rescue the sing-song girls. We used to say it was because they wanted the girls for their concubines but they didn't. I didn't unnerstand then; your grandfather had a good heart. Only my mother and my sister Mei had good hearts. I never knew a man before with a good heart. I cried and cried when he left me. The nuns sat me down and gave me some tea and I just cried. Cried for two days and didn't stop.'

La had been put to work in the convent laundry. She was safe and she was cared for.

'But I was without three things: without my child, without your grandfather and without good food.'

La could do nothing to bring back her baby and nothing, it seemed, would bring Jamie back to her.

'And the food? What could I do? The cook was what they used to call "a fallen woman".' I think she was a sing-song girl. She taught me lots of songs. But her food was horrible, not even fit for the pigs. Why didn't the nuns say anything?'

It seemed impossible to La that anyone could eat bad food without noticing. Food for her was bound up with ritual and comfort. She thought that with their communion and their rituals, the nuns would be the same. La decided that food was to be the only circumstance within her control.

'I asked the nuns if I could work in the kitchen. I said I cooked for Wang's family. I didn't. First wife wouldn't let me eat the family food. Too jealous because I had a son. She told Wang I ate like a peasant and must eat by myself. So the cook used to slip me food and I would make my Shantung dishes. Then I could remember my mother.'

She hears La's voice, slowly moving through the recipes: how to wrap dumplings, how to make stock. When she makes the food, she remembers La.

'So I helped the cook and taught her my Shantung food. At first, she laughed at me. She was from Canton. Then she asked me to cook something. Oh but she was jealous that one, all the time watching to see if I would steal her job. I just wanted good food! All I had left.'

And then he came back to La, this Jamie.

'He was sitting in the parlour with one of the nuns. I just cried and he said, "Do you want me to go?" and I shook my head. I couldn't say anything; too busy crying. I wanted to say "Take me with you" but I knew the nun would send me away. So I sat, head down and hands together, as they taught us. Then he said he was going to Scotland on a ship and first thing I thought was, "Where can I get poison to kill myself?" I was crying again and he asked me to go to Scotland with him.'

La had looked up at that.

'I just nodded. The nun said she should not have let him in but your grandfather had a way with him, you know.'

As she lights the candles in the windowsill, she wonders how it was for them when they came to the Highlands. It was always the journey north she had wanted to hear. Always La had told her, time after time of asking.

White food, red food.

La's food.

What will he bring?
Wait.
He is here.
She opens the door.
Here is the test.
A small bag.
'Open it,' he says.
Inside, a small blue and white jar.
Ginger.

Let It Be

PAUL CUDDIHY

Ah wis hawfway across the road when ah saw the car. Ah stoaped but no in time. The guy hit the brakes an the tyres pure screeched. Ah closed ma eyes. Waitin. Hopin. But the car didnae hit me. Ah stared at the guy an he stared back. Didnae eye me up an doon like they usually did. Then he held up his haun. Like it wis his fault. He waved me oan an Ah smiled. Thanks. Ah never smiled normally. No here. But it felt nice. To be treated like a human being. Ah wisnae used tae it.

The car drove away an ah watched it. No stoapin or goin slow or turnin roon the corner wi the rest ae them. Just straight oan up the hill. Gettin smaller. Smaller. Oot ae sight. Ah didnae move. Kept lookin up that hill. Ah wished ah could walk up there. Over the hill an far away. Away fae here.

A car stoaped in front ae me an the windae slid doon. Ah sighed. So much fur ma great escape.

'Lookin fur business?' Ah said. It came naturally.

'Yeah. Sure.'

'Tenner fur a haun joab. Fifteen fur oral. Twenty fur sex.'

'Eh . . . blow job.'

'Fifteen fur oral.'

'Fine.'

Ah walked roon an goat in the car. He put his windae up an started drivin.

'Do you know where to go?' he said.

'Whit?'

'Where we can do this?'

'Go doon tae the SECC. The car park there. Roon the back.'

'Alright.'

Ah could tell he wisnae used tae this. Maybe no his first time but no far aff it. Ah should ae got mair money aff him. Too late noo.

'Do you mind if I put some music on?' he asked.

'Naw.'

Whit did ah care? He pushed a button an John Lennon started singin. 'All you need is love'. Ha fuckin ha. Ah closed ma eyes. Ah loved The Beatles. It wisnae wan ae ma favourites but it wis still a magic song. Ah loved his voice. McCartney wis gid as well an 'Yesterday' makes me cry every time ah hear it but Lennon's a better singer. Naebody can argue wi that. Even ma stepda agreed an he argued aboot everythin. There wis mair emotion tae it. Like he believed every word he wis singin. Ah started hummin alang.

'You like that song?'

'It's awright.'

'Are you a Beatles' fan then?'

Ah shrugged.

'You look a bit young to remember them? What age are you?'

Ah thought about ma answer fur a second. Sometimes ah said fifteen. Some ae them liked that. Wee lassies. Pretending it wis ma first time. Sickos. But ah wisnae sure wi this guy. He looked like he might freak oot.

'Seventeen,' ah said.

'Well she was just seventeen,' he sang. Ah nodded an smiled through gritted teeth. 'Do you know that song?' he said.

'Naw,' ah lied.

'That's a Beatles song as well. One of their early ones.'

No kiddin. 'I Saw Her Standing There'. Aff the *Please Please Me* album. The very first track. The cover wi John, Paul, George an Ringo hangin over a veranda. Smilin fur the camera. Daft wee boys without a care in the world. Like they didnae know they wur about tae become the most famous people ever. Ah could ae telt him aw that but ah didnae. He pressed the button an the CD jumped tae a new song. 'Eight Days A Week'. John Lennon again. Magic.

Ah wanted tae sing alang. Belt oot the words like the way ah used tae. In ma bedroom. Singin intae ma hairbrush. Dancin in front ae the mirror. Ma maw shoutin up the stairs: 'Turn that fuckin racket doon.'

It was awright when ma stepda played it. She widnae shout at him. Widnae dare. Whit a racket that wis. Efter a night at the pub. Up full blast. Him screamin alang wi every song. Me an Ellie lyin in bed. Tossin an turnin. Until he fell asleep oan the couch.

We stoaped at a red light. The guy wis drummin his fingers aff the steerin wheel. Ah knew he wis stealin glances at me. Lookin at ma legs. Ah wisnae bothered. Some ae them tried tae touch me. Grab ma leg. Slide their hauns up ma skirt. Ah just pushed them away. Telt them tae fuck off. Wan guy grabbed ma wrist. Bent it back. Till ah thought it wis gonnae snap. Ah hud tears in ma eyes. An ah wis scared. Some ae the girls wilnae wear skirts. But ah always dae. Catches the eye. Ah always hud guid legs. Everyone said so. Ma best feature.

'Oh, I like this one,' the guy said, turnin up the volume. 'Ticket To Ride'. Lennon again. He started singin alang but ah could tell he wis nervous. His voice wis tremblin. Ah wis annoyed noo. Wi masel. Ah could ae goat a lot mair than fifteen quid. Maybe ah wid chance it. Ah didnae think he'd go psycho oan me.

'What's your name?'

'Whit?'

'What's your name?'

'Anne.'

'That's a nice name.'

So it fuckin wis. Like ah cared whit he thought aboot ma name. Like he cared. Like ah telt him ma real name. Nae kissin an nae personal stuff. They wur ma two rules. Sometimes they'd ask ma name an ah'd say whit dae you want it tae be? Jist tae see whit they'd say. Wan time this guy said 'Petula' an ah burst oot laughin. He wisnae too happy aboot that.

He'd stoaped singin. Didnae join in wi the high-pitched voices at the end. Ah tried tae guess the next song. 'Help'. If it wis that wan then ah knew whit album he wis listenin tae. *The Number*

Ones. Twenty seven ae them. Brilliant. Ellie hud goat me it fur ma Christmas. Two years ago noo. It didnae seem like it. Ah wondered whit she wis dain noo. Ah hoped she wis stickin in at school. Mair than ah did.

Ma maw said it wis the wrang crowd ah goat in wi but ah'm no blamin naebody else. Ma stepda said ma maw wis too saft wi me. Wi both ae us. But mainly me. He didnae like me cause ah stood up tae him. Cheeky bitch me. Ah widnae huv taken the shite ah gave them.

'Where do we go now?'

We were drivin alang by the river. Nearly there.

'Jist drive intae the car park an go roon the back an doon tae the end.'

'Sure.' Ah wis right aboot the album. It wisnae ma favourite but. That wis *Let It Be.* Maist people liked *Rubber Soul* or *Revolver.* Real Beatles' fans. But ah always preferred *Let It Be.* It wis a dead sad album. Like they aw knew it wis the end. In their hearts. But nane ae them wanted tae admit it. No jist yet. Ah passed a record shop the other day an noticed it wis oot again. A new version. *Naked.* It wis in the shop windae an ah stoaped an stared at it. Fur ages. Ah went in tae the shop an hud a look. Held it in ma hauns an turned it over. Front cover. Back cover. Ah noticed some ae the songs wur different fae the wan ah hud. The wan ah'd pawned alang wi aw ma other CDs. Goat aboot fifty pence fur each wan.

A wee fat security guard wi a red face an nae hair stood right beside me. Watchin. Waitin fur me tae slip it intae ma poacket. Ah didnae blame him. Ah looked like wit ah wis. A junkie. Ah put the CD back an walked oot. Ah wished ah could ae goat it. Paid fur it. Like a normal person.

The car drove by the SECC an roon the back. The guy kept lookin oot his windae or in the mirror. Waitin fur someone tae see us but naebody ever did.

'Will I go right down to the bottom there?' he asked.

'Aye. In the corner. Near they bushes.'

There wis wan other car parked in the middle ae the car park but it didnae look like there wis anybody in it. Nae windaes steamed up or nothin.

'We'll be alright here?' He wis nervous. Maybe it wis his first time?

'Aye. We'll be fine.'

He pressed the CD again. Somethin tae dae wi his hauns. Ah wis glad. Missed oot 'Yesterday'. Ah didnae want tae cry in front ae him. 'Yellow Submarine' came oan. Ma stepda's favourite. Always sang it at parties. Really badly. But naebody said anythin. Just listened an then cheered an clapped when he finished like it wis Ringo fuckin Starr himsel that hud sung it. Naebody wanted tae say that it wis shite. No jist him. But that The Beatles hud actually written a shite song.

He thought he wis the biggest Beatles' fan in the world. Ma stepda. Said he'd seen them in concert. Live. The real thing. But he wis only forty-two so he'd huv been aboot nine when they split up. An they stoaped tourin in 1966 so he'd huv been five. Bullshit. Ah never said anythin. Ah don't know if ma maw sussed him oot. If she did she nivir said anythin either.

He hud aw the albums. Vinyl. Said they wur the real thing. Fae the 1960s. But that wis bullshit tae. Ah found that oot fae the pawn.

Ma maw met him at a Bootleg Beatles concert in Glesga. In the bar. Him wi his sixties' suit. Plain grey wi nae lapels. Came up tae her an ma aunty Marie. Wi the put-on Liverpool accent. They thought he wis great. Well ma maw must huv cause he came hame that night an never left. He'd talk like that in the hoose sometimes. Tryin tae show aff. Make ma maw laugh. Make her remember when they first met. When it wis still gid. Sounded like Ringo daein the voice fur Thomas the fuckin Tank Engine tae me. It made me laugh. Behind his back.

The guy turned the engine aff but the music kept playin. Ah waited fur him tae dae somethin or say somethin but he jist kept starin oot the windae.

'Fifteen quid,' ah said.

'Oh, right. Sorry.' He goat his wallet an pulled oot the cash. There wis mair in there. Much mair. I wondered whether ah could dip him. He probably widnae even notice. Widnae be expectin it. It wis a lot ae money. Mair than ah wid get the night. Ah'd nivir done it before but some ae the girls did. Wan or two goat caught. Wisnae pretty then.

Ah took the money an stuffed it intae ma bag. Ah rummaged aboot an goat a condom. The guy started tae unzip his troosers. Slowly. He laughed. Still nervous. He pushed them doon past his knees. Ah kept an eye oan the poacket wi the wallet. Still thinkin aboot whit tae dae.

'You better move yur seat back a bit. Gie me a bit mair room,' ah ordered. He obeyed without a word. 'Penny Lane' came oan and ah knew we were almost back tae 'All You Need Is Love'.

Ah knew aw the albums aff by heart. That's aw ah hud listened tae fur years. As lang as ah can remember. Ellie liked modern stuff. Westlife an aw that boy band shite but ah wis always a mammy's girl. She liked The Beatles an so did ah. An when it wis jist the girls it wis magic. Me an Ellie an ma maw. Playin the songs an dancin aboot crazy. We always hud tae let Ellie pit wan ae her songs oan an dance aboot tae that as well. Me an ma maw wid pull faces behind Ellie's back but we still danced. Tae keep her happy. An it made me happy tae.

We nivir danced once ma stepda came tae stay. Ah don't blame ma maw. Two weans an the stretch marks tae prove it. Some fuckin catch. An the weddin wis awright. Me an Ellie were bridesmaids. Wearin these horrible lime green puffy dresses. But ma maw was beautiful. No like a princess. But she wis . . . happy. An that made her beautiful. Ma stepda wore his grey suit. It hud a beer stain oan the jaicket which widnae wash oot. The band played Lennon an McCartney aw night. An ah danced an danced. Till it wis time tae go hame tae ma granny's. Ma maw wis goin on honeymoon. A weekend in Perth. The Bootleg Beatles wur playin there an hc hud goat tickets. Ah suppose it wis kinda romantic. Then they came hame an there wis nae mair dancin.

Ah ripped the packet an pulled oot the condom. Ah put ma bag between ma knees an closed ma legs around it. Naebody wis goin tae dip me. He'd pulled his boxers doon as well an ah slipped the condom oan. He leant back in his seat an ah put ma head in his lap. He let oot a few wee moans.

I had his dick in ma mooth an ma haun oan his dosh. He wis touchin ma hair. Runnin his haun through it. An John Lennon wis singin 'There's nothin' you can do that can't be done'.

When ah wis a wee girl ma maw wid sing me tae sleep. Ah wis scared ae the dark. Even wi Ellie in the bed beside me. She wid be snorin. Fast asleep as soon as her head hit the pillow. But ah couldnae dae that. Even wi the light fae the hall creepin intae the room across the carpet. Ma maw wid sit oan the edge ae the bed. Strokin ma hair. Singin tae me in a whisper. Like ma guardian angel. Singin ma song. The wan they wrote aboot me. 'Michelle, ma belle, these are words that go together well, ma Michelle.'

Our Big Day Out

TRACEY EMERSON

Boots. Debenhams. River Island, Top Shop, Marks and Spencers.
Warehouse. Waterstone's. Baskin' Robbins. Mint Choc Chip, two
scoops and a breather. That's how I wasted the hour between 2 and
3 p.m. in the strip-lit shopping centre in the northern town I've
never been back to. You were with me. Well, I suspected you were.

Back to Boots. This time I had the courage to buy the test.

'You're a careless piece of shit and your boyfriend's a fuck-up.'
The girl at the till was direct.

'I know.' I couldn't look at her.

'Excuse me?' She sounded confused, having said none of the
above.

I took my paranoia downstairs to the food hall and paid 20
pence for the privilege of using the toilets. I unbelted then
unbuttoned my coat and gently rubbed my breasts. Relief. It
was the concrete tits that first alerted me to the chance of your
existence. Pre-menstrual tension I'd assumed, but nothing followed. They swelled, hardened, burned and insisted until I
brought us all here, me, them and the possibility of you.

I chose the end cubicle. Inside, I hung up my coat and began
preparations for the test. I was poised, the white plastic stick
expectant beneath me when a mother and son tumbled through
the main door, all screams and leg slapping.

'Want out!' The boy was wrestled into the cubicle next to mine.
Trapped. I could see tiny red wellingtons, patterned with puddle
splashing ducks.

'Shut up!' Her tone was threatening enough to buy us both a
moment's peace. Silence. An embarrassed silence, each of us
willing the other to go first. I concentrated, holding the test firmly.

Testing, testing, one, two, three. Testing, testing, time to pee. If I said it out loud would she laugh and let go? She eventually broke the deadlock.

'Mummy, mummy, mummy.' The boy laughed, the little red boots jumped up and down. Using the noise as cover, I released a heavy stream, darting the stick into it, wetting my hand. I imagined thousands of women, nationwide, pissing on their fingers. Was I the only one in a shopping centre? I read the instructions. One blue line – negative; two – positive. It would take four minutes. Four minutes from now, a silent explosion of emotions would shake our little island. Joy, anger, relief, disbelief, fear and disappointment. Waves of emotion at four-minute intervals. All day, every day. I sat, a mundane statistic, waiting for the blue lines that might predict my future.

Next door, the mother was zipping and fastening and rearranging layers. I willed the boy to crouch down and stick his cheeky face into my cubicle. Anything to make this moment memorable. 'Well, there I was, just waiting, when all of a sudden this adorable cherub of a face appeared and, well, what can I say, it was a sign.' They left, I never saw his face and at 3.39 p.m., a second blue line appeared.

I tensed for the explosion. In Edinburgh, Debbie, the Australian temp, walked in shock from the first floor toilets to her desk on the second floor and sat staring at her screensaver. She tried not to look at Dave from New Zealand who hadn't looked at her since that night in December. In Bristol, a childless woman cried with joy, hoping her husband believed in miracles and wouldn't connect this unlikely conception with the fitting of his new kitchen six weeks ago. In a shopping centre, in a town she's never been back to, a young woman told herself this didn't happen to university graduates frozen by too many opportunities.

'Which do you want?' The teenager before me didn't hide her impatience well.

'The flapjack.' It was on the plate before I saw my mistake.

'Sorry, gateaux.' She gripped the cake slice tightly, probably counting to ten. As she separated a piece from the rich, dark whole I saw my mistake. Far too big, far too sickly.

'I'm really sorry . . .' Back slid the gateaux, the girl shaking her head. The flapjack landed on the tray next to my cappuccino. We avoided eye contact for the rest of the transaction.

The food hall was circular, the brightly signed stalls ringing a raised seating area. Public art interrupted the chairs and tables; abstract sculptures to confuse the elderly and give kids a place to stuff cold chips. I sat on the sidelines, watching school children trickle in for a dose of carbonated sugar. These were pre-mobile days. If technology had overtaken us even faster, would I have rung someone, my mother, your father? Or sent a message to a friend, something flippant and life-reducing:

'UP DUFF. HELP Sx'

I needed an old lady, preferably a slightly unhinged old lady who'd come here to escape the weight of memory, gasping for conversation. She'd squeeze herself into the chair, ignoring all the empty tables around us.

'You don't mind do you dear?'

I'd shake my head and when she was settled I'd start to cry, silently, until she noticed me.

'What's wrong dear?' she'd ask.

'Everything.'

'Be specific.' She'd be tetchy, not as gentle as she looked.

'I'm pregnant.' I'd whisper, hoping the low volume might disguise the truth.

'I see.'

I'd tell her everything. That I was lonely. That I'd abandoned friends and family to stretch lust into love and domesticity with someone I shouldn't have. That our sex was indifferent. That the future wasn't a place we expected to visit together.

'So leave.' She wouldn't be the tactful type.

'It's not that easy.' I'd explain how we'd just left college, knowing who we could be but not how to get there. How we were lost in a tangle of menial jobs, benefit fraud and pseudo-nervous breakdowns. His, not mine.

'Like newborn calves,' she'd pause to cut up her scone, 'thrust into the world, slipping giddy on treacherous reality.'

'Very true.' I'd watch as she'd pick all the raisins out of the scone. 'We're the perfect excuse for each other's fear and ineptitude.'

'Quite.' She'd rearrange the raisins in a circle round the edge of her plate. I'd start to cry again. She'd look up, confused, as though seeing me for the first time.

'What's wrong dear?'

'I'm pregnant', then with the volume up, 'I'm pregnant.'

I'd spoken out loud. A few heads turned and stared, looking away when they realised there'd be no further drama. Feeling flushed I removed my black jumper, stuffing it into my backpack, then closed my eyes on the world as I'd always seen it. Lids squeezed against eyeballs until red and blue turned black and green. This was a favourite childhood game; it had passed the time while I refused to fall asleep. Hallucogenic journeys down winding stain glass passages; the colours enhanced by pressing the knuckles deep into the eye socket.

Then it happened. My two halves connected. The idea of you travelled up from my womb, solidified in my mind then shot back down again and I could actually feel you there.

I opened my eyes. Mothers and children, blurry images in my former world picture, now came sharply into focus. Around me children sat, squirmed, giggled and cried, all of them handled with varying levels of patience.

A uniformed boy preyed on the tables, feeding plastic and paper to a bin he wheeled behind him. I pushed my tray away, unintentionally luring him over. As he reached the table he stumbled and as I watched him lose his balance, I crossed my arms over my stomach and moved backwards.

'Sorry.' He took the tray away. I kept my arms where they were and you and I sat, links in the same chain, wondering who would make the first move.

I began the calculations. Doctor's appointment first, for confirmation. He'd give me time to think. I'd wait an acceptable two days to show I'd struggled with it, then return and set the inevitable in motion.

I'd tell your dad as soon as I got home. I could never keep dramatic news to myself, especially when I had the starring role.

I turned and placed both wrists on the chrome railing that penned in the diners. Cool and soothing, it slowed down the life speeding through me. Next to my right hand, stray strands of tinsel lay trapped under scraps of cellotape. The remnants of Christmas clung to the shopping centre. Ripped streamers dangled from ceilings, the wires once strung with twirling snowflakes and fairy lights hung still and empty.

We didn't have much time. Leaving the food hall we headed for Waterstone's.

'Excuse me,' I interrupted a man stacking shelves, 'I'm trying to find something for my little one.'

I followed him to the children's section with its pink sofa and soft toys. I found us a book about a frog and another about a caterpillar, which we sat down and read.

'Any joy?' The assistant again, eager to please.

'Have you got anything for six- to eight-week-olds?' He took his time to think about it, puzzled.

'Umm, sorry, no.'

We toured the bookshop. I showed you the books I'd like to have given you. My favourites, *Robinson Crusoe*, *Arabian Nights*, *Little Women* and all of Enid Blyton. That took us a while.

'I've still got most of these,' I explained, 'I must've kept them for you.'

We moved onto 'Mind, Body, Spirit'. I'd spent hours in there, looking for answers. Your Dad said I had so many self-help books I should build myself a den out of them, curl up inside and never come out.

It was hot in this cosy shoppers' nest. I pulled off the first of two long-sleeved tops and tied it around my waist.

Next was 'Theatre and Film'. I told you how auditions worked and showed you the Ophelia speech I used when I went to them. Naturally you wanted to visit the 'Mother and Baby' section, full of bumpy women glowing and browsing. We looked at pictures of developing babies, cord-tied to the womb, so you could see what you might have looked like.

'Are you okay?' An older woman with grey roots, obviously mature enough to staff this precious section, looked at us, concerned.

'We're fine thanks.' I slipped the book back into its alphabetical home.

'Do you want a tissue?'

'Are you sure?'

Back in the foyer, I leant on the railings and looked down at the food hall. You were getting restless. Your boredom irritated me.

I was trying my best. If we'd had more time I'd have shown you where I came from. We'd visit the village I grew up in. We'd walk through the woods where I kissed all of my boyfriends. It was a ritual. I'd take them to the bridge over the Roman river where we'd kiss, cuddle and probe. I took your Dad there. I could have declared it the site of your conception. Would you have known I was lying? Only going home would mean seeing my mother, who'd unlock me as only she could.

Here our parting could be swift and anonymous.

Mothercare was on the ground floor. How sensible. Full of sensible people choosing sensible equipment for their new, grown-up hobby. I wandered around, touching towelling and rubbing pink-quilted fabrics against my cheeks. I took a pair of maternity dungarees into the changing-room.

'What do you think?' We howled at the sight of me and I

pretended to be a woman from a Weight Watcher's ad, doing the before and after pictures.

As I left the cubicle, a Japanese woman was turning side to side in front of a long mirror, modelling the same dungarees we'd found so amusing.

'How do they look . . . honestly?'

'Honestly?' I hated this type of changing-room encounter with its instant intimacy.

She laughed, 'An unsightly necessity.'

I laughed with her. She nodded at the dungarees I was carrying.

'You're organised' She searched for evidence of you in my still flat stomach.

'It's my first.' Would that satisfy her?

She smiled. 'This is my second.'

'Congratulations.'

'I lost my first.'

Going up the escalator I worried we'd left too hastily. You didn't think so. We agreed it was a shame for the woman. A faint stream of cold air led us upwards, from subterranean safety to a day already dark. We stopped at the main doors, the metal handles a thermometer for the cold outside. Beyond the glass was January, the New Year gestating. I untied my top and slipped it back on.

You weren't quite ready to leave yet. I said we'd seen all there was to see but you demanded I turn around and find . . . I wasn't sure what. You led me back down to the food hall, making me stand in front of the burger bar until the smell of chips and frying meat reeled me in. My ten-year dedication to vegetarianism didn't bother you. Up at the counter I struggled with the menu. This was an unfamiliar routine, not practised since teenage days. Letting you choose was liberating. No decisions, no responsibility.

'Cheeseburger and chips . . . and a large coke.'

It was beautiful. Every last grease-sodden mouthful. The onions, the gherkins, the ketchup, the cheap char-grilled meat. All of it. The burger bar was popular with children. We sat and watched them eating, their volume and activity increasing with every mouthful. I imagined you wriggling around, high on your additive fix.

The centre was getting busier. After-workers trailed around the January sale circuit, knowing the real bargains were gone but desperate for a souvenir from this warm little world full of glitter and promise. We walked in and out of shops, watching them rummage through creased and sweat-stained clothes, spoiled with traces of other people's longing. I tried to explain the enjoyment in spending money you don't have on things you don't need but I couldn't.

On the way to the main entrance you spotted a photo booth. I had change and it would only take five minutes. Inside we argued over the backdrop until I gave in and pulled the orange curtain over the blue. We stayed sitting for the first two flashes, then I tried to balance on the stool to get my midriff in the frame. We laughed at that third photograph, a snapshot of my arm and back as I stopped myself from falling. I stared at myself in the first two pictures, a serene and complete animal, worry replaced by certainty and purpose.

The glass doors again. I put the black jumper on. Our big day out was over.

Coat next. I was glad of my coat, an impulse buy from a retro clothing shop in London. I felt special when I wore it. I checked the pockets. Hat in the left, gloves in the right. I slowly fastened the buttons, burying you under soft red layers. As I finished doing up the coat, a man approached from outside, face twisted at the weather. He saw me by the doors and, in an old-fashioned gesture, held them open. He smiled but was impatient to get inside. Finally the belt. I pulled it tight, tighter than it needed to be, tight enough to sever the connection between the top and bottom of my body.

Joy

CELAEN CHAPMAN

She was so painful, a long labour. I think we hate each other for that. She's just a strange baby, blank, and hardly cries or laughs, just watches thin air all the time. All I can think is, I have to keep myself guarded because today is the first day. I have been driving since five this morning and I haven't got myself sorted yet. I have to leave her in the car. It's a colder day than yesterday; I spread my duvet out in the boot, folded double, put her on top, wearing most of her clothes, and cover her in a wool blanket. For her size it must be like sleeping in a double bed. If it were me, I'd get claustrophobic. I'm sure this is OK; it has taken me a while to work out where to park, because if she starts crying on a quiet street, or in a multi-storey, someone will hear her. So I find a place not too far away, next to the feeder road for the motorway. It's noisy and hardly anyone walks that way because there's no pavement, just smoothed round stones half sunk into concrete. I have thought about this; it's close enough I can get out every couple of hours to check, and I parked the car facing the road, with its back at the fire escape. There are windows, in parts of the building no-one uses so I will be able to check without anyone noticing.

The building is eight floors high and runs the length of the whole street. It was a canned food factory before, and it still looks cavernous. I'm at the entrance before the security guard has finished puffing his first cigarette. I need a pass with my photograph on it, and he only smiles when he suggests that I should pose topless for mine. He uses a Polaroid camera, me standing against the whitewashed wall while people who already have passes walk past. Further in I start mapping the insides of the building. Past reception, there are two old lifts with dull metal doors. There's a seventies' stairwell, with square turns, shiny green linoleum.

The office is on the fifth floor, high enough for good views, but not so high it will feel desolate. I have already worried about this. (But later in the kitchen I notice that the water in the sink gently moves when the building is hit by the north wind.) I am in the lift with an engineer – it can only carry the weight of five people – then it's full, so even with two it's close. After the stomach dip, the doors stay closed; I can smell the thick grease on the engineer's yellow jacket. He's been looking at me, maybe I look crazy, so I make a small smile. In the first seconds I'm running fast films in my head about what will happen if we are here all day with the doors not opening, or all night until tomorrow. I will have to phone my brother and tell him about the car. Then the engineer swears before I say anything. He says, well, that's us in here for an hour. I hope you're not one of those people who gets panicky in lifts. And he uses his mobile to call his office. On the eighth floor the hatch to the lift gear room is padlocked, the security guard has a key, but there is also a spare key on the top step of the access ladder, plugged down with blue tack. I overhear this, and also that half of the building has been empty for nine years. A lot of dead space to be lost in, and I think I can try and live here until I'm sorted. The engineer says it will only take an hour to get us out.

At lunchtime I use the cleaners' kitchen to sterilise the bottle; they only work later in the afternoon, and the rest of the day it's empty. When I get down to the car, I lift her up, put her in the baby seat and sit next to her in the back. She's hungry, she sucks at the bottle, holding the glass with two sticky hands. She smells bad, but I don't want to change her in the car; I hate the smell, and it will be worse in a small space. It takes about half an hour for her to drink everything.

This time I climb the stairs. I know the engineers have gone, because the hatch at the top of the access ladder is padlocked. I find the key; I'm nervy because the ladder is just next to the lift, but I'm lucky. The hatch down to the empty section is not locked. When I get back to the office, someone asks where I went for lunch, trying to be nice because it's my first day. I say I had to go to the post office. I smile; I'll have more time to talk to the people here later. I leave with everyone else at five, then I get my new key copied, buy nappies, bread, baby milk, curry for the microwave. Whisky. After six the security guard leaves and I use my new pass to open the doors. I carry her in the car seat, and when I meet one of the cleaners I explain that I have left my purse upstairs. When she fusses over the baby I don't say anything.

I have to not imagine what could be on other floors below me, or in some of the rooms that I walk past that have been locked. The lights work – I tried them earlier – but after dark I have to use the light from the motorway outside. The heating is on very low, probably to keep back the worst of the damp, although everywhere the walls are peeling. In some of the rooms windows are broken or missing, but most of them are boarded, which means someone must check. The layout doesn't make any sense: narrow corridors, halls, small offices, some machinery. I find a disused canteen that must have been big enough to feed a few hundred people. It was cleaned before it was closed, but there is no gas, and the taps are dry. It feels hollow. At the back of the canteen I find a small room, with a side door out to one of the narrow corridors. There are two ways to get out if I need to. There are blinds covering half of the window, enough to shelter me, and let in light from outside. I make a cot for her by pushing together two office chairs. I also find shelves, an old radio and a couch, like in a doctor's surgery, that I can sleep on. It'll do for a while.

At night, late, I don't want to hear or see the weather, instead I shut my eyes and listen to the underground; the sound rumbling up through the concrete and girders, like noise through a bone. I'm here because I am sick of fields, but this morning, driving into the city, I can see all these buildings, close together; trees growing between the dual carriageway, leaves are caught in the drains, so that water swells wide and floods the road. Gulls circle the sheer sides of the tower blocks. I feel like the fields are seeping in beside me and I stop looking. Instead I think about the smell, there is a new one every few minutes; the flavour of a car exhaust, how it's different to the bus that follows; then there's sick, perfume, curry, bread, the sticky smell from the distillery. She just sits in the back of the car blinking at all the lights. I want to love all this like it's mine.

She has been crying a bit tonight, but it gets better after I feed her. God knows where the moon is. I drink capfuls of whisky until I start to relax, but just then, I press my hand against the window and my skin feels frozen. Like the grass near Peerie Voe when it freezes, when the blades are thick and sappy at the core but the skin is glass brittle. Like an insect. The window is wet with condensation, water breathed out by us; snow is driving down from above the lights, the flakes are thin as dust, so as they move they show the shape of the wind. Everything gets closer; the distance between my hand and the black windows on the other side of the motorway can be spanned by the spaces between snow flakes. A crow flies past, silent, and looks me in the eye.

Then I must be drunk because I forget to blink. I'm imagining myself out of range. My favourite escape, as if I have just dived into a pool, but instead splash-land in the middle of the sea. Three miles above my head a satellite is crawling a neat line through the stars. Past the blackest point in the distance, the sea spreads one hundred miles north to Shetland. Balancing on my horizon I can see the lights of tankers, long-range fishing boats, klondykers, passing miles off in a shipping lane. The same as the satellite. But inside one, a man will be drinking beside shelves of lashed-down videos. Or a woman will be sitting writing an e-mail. Everyone else on the ships will be sleeping, rocked, if I squeeze my eyes together I can imagine that I am making the waves.

I'm leaving her with you. Not an evil thing to do because she'll cry too much and I can't be there all the time. I never wanted a baby; she's not mine, we don't belong to each other. But she is my daughter. Take her back north with you. The house at Peerie Voe will be a better shape for her, fit her better. I'll send the money. Mum and Dad will help. I'll write a letter soon. She was born on the ninth of October. Call her Joy – she looks like her Gran.

When his sister called, he was in his flat in Glasgow, preparing to leave for his grandmother's funeral, and for home, the next day. He had been living there for five years; three at university, then two working, earning good money, thinking he would settle. But then his grandmother died. His Mum phoned him at work, just minutes afterwards; her voice sounding small. The first picture he saw in his mind, while his Mum was still talking, was a photograph of his Gran.

On his last long visit, three summers ago, he had stayed at her house for nearly a week; they sat together into the early hours, drinking, writing on the backs of the photographs, sometimes just names, sometimes more. *Gran, on the beach at St Ninian's, aged sixteen, taken by Al, we had just started courting.* In the picture she is laughing, holding her skirt down with one hand, holding a cigarette with the other; she is in love. Or: *Da and me, my first time on the water*, written on the back of the only photograph of her father; fierce eyes, standing on his boat, his only daughter standing in front of him, aged about five, in shorts, mesmerised by the camera. But the photograph he saw clearest before he started thinking about leaving for home, was the colour photograph, him at eight, standing with his Gran, both of them grinning. He could feel the beach at midnight, in the simmer dim, oystercatchers squealing just out of the frame, the warmth of his Gran's hands on his shoulders. His grandfather's house at Peerie Voe would be empty. For the rest of the day he couldn't work. He stared through the window at the sky, watching the haunted weather course down from the North Sea.

The baby wasn't unexpected. Him ending up with the baby wasn't unexpected. He had met his sister off and on for the last five years; she moved all the time, living in various places, never for very long, and most of the time drinking too much. She wasn't well; she had a strange lucidity, she would stare at him and tell him immaculate stories. He remembered the last one; she was walking in a park, and a stranger, a man, had given her a suitcase of money, thousands of pounds, he said, because she looked so beautiful. She told him she was hiding the money and would one day give all of it to him. The last time he had met her for only a few hours, she had just left hospital; she had wide blue plasters on all the fingers of her left hand. She told him that she had been working in a restaurant and had scalded them. A week earlier the consultant explained that she had carefully peeled away the fingerprints on her left hand with a scalpel, then punched through the window of a newsagent. When she was in the hospital she didn't recognise him. After that meeting she disappeared again; she was always untraceable. She had a mobile phone, but was careful about when and where she used it. It was almost always off, but phoning it two or three times a day had become a habit for all of them. The baby was born a few months ago, she had called home to tell them. She was in the Borders, there would be a public christening, hundreds of people at the cathedral, so she said, but she didn't invite anyone.

She was slurry. He told her about the funeral, that he planned to move into the house at Peerie Voe. He offered to pay for her and the baby to travel back with him. None of the family had seen the baby yet. Usually, she switched her phone off before he had finished talking, but instead she was quiet, and then said 'Yes, I'll come. I'll come to your flat tonight. Don't go out, I'll go with you. I'll be there in two hours.' She was always precise. But instead when he opened the door, his sister's baby was staring up at him from the pavement. She was pressed into a carrier, and there was an envelope tucked under one of the safety straps, his first name written on it in large letters. The baby was very small. He took her into the house and lifted her out of the carrier. She was tiny. She still stared at him, wouldn't take her eyes off him, and then started screaming as if she had been holding a storm in her lungs. He held her, and didn't put her back into the carrier, or read the letter until she was asleep. She wore exactly the same expression as her great Gran in the photograph of the boat. Her eyes were the same colour as the winter sea at dawn.

There was a tannoy announcement, barely audible against the wind, warning there would be swell after the boat turned the corner of Orkney. It is a white boat, thirty years' weight of paint, and the wide steel sheets of its sides are dented. There are orange places where rust has mixed in like a dye. Only the lowest outside deck is accessible; the two higher decks have been roped off because of the wild weather. He keeps his line of vision straight as the boat rolls, to a string of rigs, hard lights in the distance. He is standing at the stern, in the sheltered envelope behind the exhaust funnel. It is late dark, just before dawn; he can still see the clotted trail of fumes, knocked out to an angle by the wind. He is holding the baby wrapped close in soft covers. Every few minutes she struggles like a cat. It has surprised him how easy it is to take on the role of guardian; how he continues to be, with each sequence of events, completely overwhelmed by the desire to keep her safe. For example, here on deck, he feels a fringe of horror when he imagines dropping her into the sea, just walking the few steps to the low railing, holding her out, and letting go. Before she hits the water he can see her covers being sucked away by the wind.

As he unlocks the door he can hear the weather forecast, the clear voice muffled by the sea. The radio has been on in the empty house all through the winter. The lights are out; she had switched some off, and others have burned out, but the walls feel warm when he touches them and it is a brilliant white day. He opens the windows to let in the sound of the gulls. Her favourite room had always been the kitchen, because of her father's oak table, and the view over to the skerries. He smiles, lifts Joy out of the carrier and walks to the window. Joy looks up at him, then looks towards the light, opening and closing her small fists in the air.

Aurora Borealis

KENNETH SHAND

Her name was Aurora Borealis. She showed me bruises she thought were beautiful, in reds and greens and blues, and though I thought I loved her, I never knew her well.

She began like the alphabet: ABC, Aurora Borealis Christensen. In Aberdeen Hospital in 1983. On the 11th of May, the day the city's only team won the European Cup. In Gothenburg, where her gran lived.

The name goes back further to a school in Sweden where her mother stared at photographs of celestial phenomena and mouthed the Latin words. They were lovely words; they grew on her tongue and germinated until a game of children's names cemented them in place. The names the other girls chose meant nothing; she was too cool for Agnetha or Anni-Frid, Benny or Björn. She wanted a name that meant something. That night in bed she imagined she was lying beneath a broad dark sky, filled with iridescent colour, and made a little prayer.

Aurora always bruised easily. It started the day her father began two weeks onshore in the pub, watching a football match with the feigned enthusiasm of a disinterested foreigner. At half-time as the pies came round, he walked out on a premonition, soaked up a grey city made a sea of red, hailed a taxi and headed home. There he found an empty house and a note from his neighbour, alerting him to the imminent birth. So it was that at the ninetieth minute Aurora's father found himself marching through ward after ward, surrounded by the screaming of little boys about to be given names like Alex or Willie or Eric. Then, just as a wayward free-kick won and lost a football match, he heard his wife straining against the last of her contractions and called out, pushing through a partition curtain and distracting the midwife (a jittery woman on a diet of slimming pills and black coffee), causing something of a flawed delivery as Aurora fell, a breath old, to bruise for the very first time.

The first time I remember Aurora was when they tightened up on school uniform, and asked the girls to wear dresses or skirts. She came in wearing a plaited mini-skirt over a pair of lime green tights. All assembly the boys kept glancing round, as though they'd never thought of her that way before; as a focus of adolescent fantasies to be sized up and compared. They scratched their necks, tied their shoelaces, glanced furtively round. The girls looked round too, with a mixture of curiosity and disapproval. Perhaps it was this diversion of attention from the serious issues of the day (a carriage clock donated, a student teacher applauded, a broken sink) that caused the headmaster, a Mr Atkins, to lose his temper, and demand loudly, to the whole school at once, froth gathering on his upper lip, that Aurora stop wearing those outrageous tights. There was a stillness for a moment. An overhead projector whirred, a fridge hummed. A microphone fed back slightly through an old PA. One by one, everyone in the room turned to look at Aurora. They expected her to break into tears, but she didn't. She stood up slowly, kicked off her shoes, pulled the tights off leg by leg and left them in a heap, like a shed skin. A roomful of people stared guiltily at the dark bruises that stretched across her calves and up around her knees. They never made her wear a skirt again.

Aurora never did sports. She had a note from the doctor saying she didn't have to, so she ended up in the library instead, reading books about world records and pointless inventions. I twisted my knee once trying to balance on a football, and had to do the same. It was a Friday, so I got to watch the rest of the class doing cross-country in the rain while reading about the world's heaviest man. It made me wonder how the world's second heaviest man might have felt. It was likely he'd find relationships difficult, gymnastics impossible, see-saws unsatisfying. There was only one way he could counteract the problems caused by his obesity, and that was to become the very best, the world record-holder. I wondered if he'd started training himself up at an early age, shovelling down pork-rinds and cheese-steaks, deep fried pizzas and lard pie fritters, accompanied by masses of greasy chips and viscous stout. Had gone for gold, pulled out the stops. Only to come second. Pipped at the post by Jeremiah Gibbs of South Carolina, in a competition fixed by ruthless management. And what if our hero returned home from the weighing disconsolate but gracious in defeat, fell through a weak staircase and plunged to his death. And though in his lifetime he was never recognised as such, the autopsy revealed that he had, after all, been the world's heaviest man. I asked Aurora what she thought.

'He wasn't doing it for other people, you know. Look at him. The world's heaviest man. It's not an achievement. It's an illness. Maybe the second heaviest is the lucky one, because he doesn't have his photo there.'

'Yeah. He's sort of disgusting, isn't he?'

'I don't want to look at him.' Still, she kept staring until I closed the book, pulling her arms in close to her body like a contortionist trying to escape. She looked at me intently, through me. I felt like I'd said something stupid.

'Well, maybe not disgusting. That's the wrong thing to say.'

'It's how you felt.'

She rubbed her neck absentmindedly and I noticed it darkening, like an apple when it's sliced.

'Your name. It's quite unusual.'

'It's something that happens in the sky. My mum thought the words were pretty.'

Like Aurora's mother, I became fascinated with the northern lights, though I didn't get the chance to see them until 1997, the same year a cat called Snowbie was declared the world's longest at 103 cm, and Aurora kissed me for the very first time. The lights were disappointing. My parents dragged me out and told me it was the last chance I'd have to see them. We stood there at a vantage point overlooking a golf course and an amusement arcade. Smoke rose up from a power station, joining the banks of cloud above us as the flashing lights of the big dipper joined with the city's orange glow. Somewhere beyond all that, an interference with the sun's rays caused the atmosphere to ripple into sheets of bright and beautiful colour, but all that was lost on me. My parents did this all too often, like when they made me watch TV because they thought it was the last time I'd be able to hear whale song, or the spectacular waste of sleep that accompanied a lunar eclipse. The kiss was a dare in a woodwork class, performed while the teacher was outside smoking a cigarette and visualising a solid pine locomotive he was making for his son. Everyone knew I fancied Aurora by that point. I was nervous and I didn't like the idea of doing something like that as a dare, but I was worried she'd be offended if I didn't. I took it to be a bad kiss as opposed to a proper one; it was surprisingly wet and our teeth rubbed together. Aurora kept her eyes closed and smiled.

'Thank you.' One of the other boys elbowed me afterwards.

'She never thanks me.' I wanted to give him a dead arm but the teacher came back. We spent the rest of the afternoon making little cars that wobbled down ramps and fell off the sides, but the whole time I was watching Aurora. Her lips had purpled as though she'd had a bag of wine gums and she had to be excused for a nosebleed. That day I walked her home, as I sometimes did. We lived near each other, in houses described as new despite being generations old. The kiss gave me confidence.

'I'd like to ask you something, Aurora.'

'Yes?'

'Do you think I'll ever be your boyfriend?'

'You are my friend.'

'No, I mean do you think we'll ever go out?'

'It depends what you mean by that.'

'Well. You know.'

'I don't think I do.'

She'd rolled up her sleeves and was watching her arms as we walked, turning them like barbeque skewers. Something seemed to occur to her.

'Hit me.' She put her bag down and stood as if to brace herself.

'Hit me.' There was a slightly manic edge to her voice. I couldn't do it. I didn't want to hurt her. I wanted to protect her. She unhooked her rucksack and left it by her feet, then punched her own arms, until they came out green and purple, and dark shades of blue.

'Look.' She laughed as she watched them swell up. 'They're crazy, aren't they?'

I never went out with Aurora at school. I never went out with anyone at school, and I don't think Aurora did either, though every time I saw a boy pursue her I felt a surge of possessiveness. Our walks home stopped as Aurora started getting lifts from cars with boys in short-sleeved shirts and girls with too much eye make-up. Aurora started dying her hair, different shades to match her clothes, and going out to nightclubs I could never have gotten in to. We did different classes, moved in different strata within the hierarchies of the school. She was popular but distant, while I tried too hard to fit in. Wore the blandest clothes, and listened to the bands represented on the common-room walls. It was Aurora's paradox that though her skin would bruise at the slightest contact, she was more or less impervious to emotional stresses. She brushed off insults easily and didn't look for attention, but always had a cache of followers. By our final year we were living in different worlds entirely. Of this last period at school, one event stands out in particular, recorded in a piece of photographic evidence my parents kept. It commemorates the school centenary. That day Mr Atkins made us drag out benches and dinner tables, plastic chairs and foam sit-up mats. He made us stand in a field behind the school, improbably balanced on a series of the above, in order to have the whole population captured in one big photograph. I stood directly behind Aurora, and I've always believed that of all the smiling, acned faces, braces glinting in the cold dull day, ours stood out the most. The rickety bench I stood on kept on torquing against the fold of a formica table that held Aurora, the bench and me, setting me off at an angle so I teetered on the edge. The final cut has me looking down towards the mud of the playing field with an expression of total panic. Aurora, meanwhile, is caught looking up and to the side, a slight frown of concentration, as though focusing on something else entirely. I've always treated that photograph as material evidence that we bonded at school, as two dents in an otherwise orchestrated composition. In recent years, though, I've begun to question that assumption, looking behind every smile for evidence of awkwardness and unease. The closer one looks, the more obvious it is that only Aurora really stands out. Every other face betrays its insecurities. There may well be negatives that have me smiling with the rest, rejected for other flaws, but I imagine Aurora stood out in all of them. She seems remarkably detached from her surroundings. I, on the other hand, was fed up. I was sick of Saturday evening television, and suburban life at home. I was sick of being stuck there and not being able to drive. I was sick of rubbish weekend jobs and not being allowed to drink. I was sick of Aberdeen, and left it when I could.

I came home once, for Christmas. I was looking for shops I could get presents in when I stumbled upon a small but fascinating museum. There, among mummified Egyptians and massive rotating toys I found Aurora, staring at a tiny Chinese foot in formaldehyde. She traced its contours in the misted glass, and drew my curiosity. We recognised each other with a mutual delay, and I noticed her Aberdeen Cultural Services badge. She gave me a tour of the exhibits, a decaying freak show of abnormal bodies and vintage paraphernalia, stopped in front of a massive femur, and told me about its origins.

'That bone belonged to a man they called the Irish giant, the world's tallest when this place was built. William Hartford, a cotton trader and founder of this museum, was obsessed with abnormality, and wanted him for his collection. So he went across and offered him a small fortune for his skeleton after death. The giant declined, so Hartford offered his family – two sons and a wife of unremarkable height – a sort of primitive life insurance. He promised they would be well looked after if they could talk him round. He offered but they declined, thinking it would be a desecration of his body and an insult to his soul. Twice, three times, Hartford took the boat to Ireland and asked the giant personally, but he wouldn't give his bones up after death. Then, as his health deteriorated, and Hartford's fingers began to twitch, the Irish giant had his will specify that he must be buried at sea and that no-one but a direct relative should have access to his body.'

'So his family betrayed him? I mean if this bit's in here . . .'

'No. They didn't. But Hartford was obsessed. He payed trawlermen to go out and search the sea-bed. Every day for a month they cast down anchor after anchor, net after net, until they had the skeleton. This bit's the best preserved but we have the rest.'

'That's horrible.'

I watched Aurora as her eyes flickered, analysing, dissecting the exhibit. It's strange that though I remember much about Aurora; the shape of her mouth, the arrangement of freckles round her eyes and nose, I don't remember what colour her eyes were. Whether they were green or blue or aquamarine, or changed with the shades of her hair.

The two of us went out drinking, to a horror themed bar. We drank cocktails out of test-tubes and talked about people who, it turned out, neither of us knew that well. We compared the presents we'd bought and tried to decide whether a stuffed womble was better or worse than an agate slice. The pace changed round us, eventually, as trays of deep-fried delicacies scooted past, the Christmas rock music faded out, and the pub quiz began. We called our team the inflatable clockwork monkeys. That was my sole contribution to the contest, and the only round we didn't win. Aurora's knowledge was astonishing. She knew the capitals of imaginary countries, the dimensions of unquantifiable concepts, the chart positions of all manner of disposable pop songs. All those double shifts in the library seemed to have paid off. We won easily and were presented with a crate of low-alcohol beer. That night I walked Aurora home, the first time since school. I wanted to put my arm around her, but our prize kept both arms busy. That wasn't the only problem, though. The whole walk home the feeling grew that somehow we'd failed to connect. When we got to her doorstep we divvyed up the beers, hesitated for a moment and promised to keep in touch. It was the last time I saw her.

There's one more event that springs to mind when I think of Aurora. It's lodged itself there and won't be shifted. It's from a day I walked her home from school and we saw a young woman knocked over. She started crossing just as we reached the other side, left the kerb at a jogging pace. Simultaneously a white van, neglecting to signal, turned down an ambiguous junction and made contact, sending her flying ten feet or so, with a noise like a lift door shutting. It's plagued me since, that noise, and for days after cars and vans seemed like nauseating mechanical insects, dangerous and illogical. The worst thing about it was that Aurora didn't seem to register the event at all, just kept walking as though she'd been distracted by a magpie or a squirrel, or a distant firework. I hesitated as people crowded round and tapped their phones, tried to see past them, but I couldn't. It bothers me somehow that I'll never know if that woman lived or died, though I checked for flowers all week and none appeared.

I saw a montage photograph of an Aberdeen dream team once, created in honour of the club centenary and cup anniversary. Players' heads are pasted on from different years, so that spiky 1980s' mullets vie with severe 1920s' side partings. Monochromatic heads are stuck on bodies dressed in red; the whole photograph a triumph of impossible combination. Alec Ferguson's caught flashing an uncharacteristic smile as he stands by his gloriously atemporal team. The photograph made me think of another photograph, the one that reminds me of Aurora, and somehow neither one seems real anymore.

I've seen the northern lights now. Really seen them. They flared up one night as I sat in my room. I saw them through a velux window, snaking across the sky like a Chinese dragon's tail, stark and ethereal. They lit up the sky for a little while, then disappeared.

I think of Aurora less and less these days, and wonder what we'd say if we met again. Maybe nothing. When I think of her, I sometimes think the worst – that we'll meet one day and she'll have completely forgotten me.

The Weight of the Earth and the Lightness of the Human Heart

LINDA CRACKNELL

There's a body on the hill. It's not dead yet, but lying very still. I might have taken it for a victim of your cold blast, your deathly grasp. But on the eve of Beltane, your powers are sunk too low to squeeze with your bony fingers at a human neck. Now the body's on so obscure a heathery ledge that your ice-sharp eyes won't pick at it, not without my help. Even the herons that creak along behind you will miss it in this smear of fog and night.

There's something strange about its position, one arm splayed awkwardly above its head. The man refuses to move, even to curl himself into the plastic survival bag he has carried for half a lifetime. At the bottom of his rucksack, the bag is rolled against a sediment of oatcake crumbs. Their gradations enumerate his hillwalking years – last season's gravel rattles amongst earlier deposits, now ground to a fine sand. But he refuses to move. And so the rucksack pushes up his shoulder blades, thrusting his chest in a barrel to the sky, increasing the elegant curve of that arm that sinks back into the dripping moss. He seems to await the end.

I watched his progress – how the body was slowed to fumbling by lack of food, and the whisky that burned from flask to empty belly. How he slipped on the rocks of the ridge and allowed himself to slither and then pitch, thwacking rocks on the descent. Perhaps you heard, whilst wheeling this season's last circles on the wings of my winds? The weight carried him down with no resistance. He fell like the massive exhalation of a sigh, perhaps with a grain of surprise at the power with which the earth pulled him down to it, reclaiming him. 'Take me, then,' he said, and fell, easily, to obscurity.

The man remains inside the body, but he teeters between

clinging on and escape. He sinks into the bog, its dark juices oozing around him. Each groan releases him deeper under the mantle of night. He is slipping into oblivion.

Shriek with your dying laughter if you must, but if we took a hammer and chisel to this man, you might understand the weight of human cares. We would reveal the hidden landscape, the hardness that dictates his crust. Come look, put down your staff. Chip down through the strata of sadnesses, and see here, in this black seam, as if laid down by a melting glacier, the friend recently buried by liver cancer. There's the soft-eared terrier, his walking companion, crushed under a Salvesen truck. Go deeper and find the lover left behind in Turkey when he was a young man; the father who died in his second year. This layering of pains, these strata, are what make up the man. Like the earth, he is created from the inside.

Notice now (come closer, you're not so weak yet) how this final addition, like the topmost weighty stone placed carelessly on a cairn, threatens to topple the order of the rest. Bearable pains cease to be so. His sadnesses, which have seemed individual, some not even realised, now connect underground like mycelium, fastening together into a cloak which wraps the man, not warming him, but immobilising his limbs and paralysing his heart. This is what has brought the man here, for you to claim if you will, in your last glacial gasp.

And this one addition to his pains? The woman, Marion, has gone from him.

Strange, how he allows the memory of a smell to haunt him. I followed him back through the years to discover something she sprayed to glisten her arms. The fresh scent trailed after her, wafted by her hands, and he was mesmerised by the bittersweet astringency. It reminded him of hippy oils that coiled around the rooms of adolescent parties. I've seen men intoxicated, numbed by your rimey strokes till they speak slurred nonsense. But this was a human enchantment.

'It's just moisturiser,' she told him, 'but it keeps midgies away too. Those boys use it, working on the Skye Bridge, with the hard hats and beefy biceps. Nancies, eh?' But far from repelling him, it drew him close. To him, this fractional, human, rush of him to her, the miniature violence of their embraces, was a continental waltz. He felt the force of their collision, as one that thrusts the earth into mountainous buckles and folds.

And now. It happens to all of them, once they've accumulated the rocks and boulders of the years. Like this man, they are pulled into the soil by the weight of pain. They reach a balance between life and a dwindling, seeping, letting-go. They will return to the bog, a release with nothing but a small show of bubbles.

He wasn't like our normal hillwalkers, the ones you crackle after, eyeing for opportunity. I saw how the keeper, who opened the gate for him at the start of the walk (to him, another world ago) looked at him with approval. He noted the corrugated boots, decent gear for the hill, the rucksack suggesting preparedness. He registered the knowing way the man orientated his map and compass. The keeper swatted at a black cloud of midgies around his head as he said, 'The buggers are here already, aye, so early in the season.' He gestured at the damp shroud submerging the tops, and told him how 'they're lurking up there too, waiting'.

As the cuckoo called behind them, the keeper watched the man with the map. His finger crossed the lines which spread and angled and lay against each other to describe this rocky place. How foolish of them not to see the slim shard of time it represents. The lines on the map gesture towards past petrifactions, bubblings and foldings. But they give up no trace of the shifts and rifts to happen tomorrow.

Then the keeper saw the man put the map away in his pocket, slide the red arrows on his compass to lay one over the other, and march away on zero degrees, not even on the path.

I watched him, long after the keeper had turned away to his work on the estate. So you see, my bony-shouldered friend, it was as if I drew him on, sucking him towards me with my strong-muscled cheeks. The compass was back in his pocket, but he walked on, as if the orientation was hard-wired in his brain, like an arctic tern migrating north in summer, following the daylight to my realm.

He waded blaeberry and bog cotton, his boots clattering across your deep-clawed scratches on the limestone pavement. His head was bent to some human pilgrimage of despair that I was unable to interpret. Like the salmon, sniffing its way back up-river to its birthplace through the familiar sequence of reversed smells – pine-perfumed currents, granite flavoured ground-water, soft sediments – he seemed to discern his path. Do not ask me why he came so desperately towards me. No, it's not for me to know everything, not every small thing, my dear.

He noticed the puddles lying in moats around moss-lined rocks, and he saw, reflected in the sleek surface, the clouds that scudded across them. This was all the puddles gave him at the beginning. He climbed higher, into the mist, a black speck against white where he crossed the snow pockets still clutched jealously by the wrinkles of the hill, just as you cling to the months of ice. Then the reflection of the sky was lost to the bog pools, and he looked deeper.

It was faint at first to him, just the hinted arc of an eye-socket. He drank whisky from his flask and saw the dull embossed band across the forehead of one, and at the next, the faint shape of rusted shutters across the chest and over the shoulders, protecting the heart. This he knew to be exactly the defence he should have had. I saw him laugh at this thought, slow and stumbling, and his hands flapped at his open coat as if in an attempt to close himself against your parting gusts. A slight shiver shook at him.

Head to toe, caged foot to cased elbow, heads butted up against each other, he saw the brotherly warriors waiting under the bog. He saw that the metallic scales would still clink if they rose out of the bog and were shaken, like the terrier sprinkling water from its

The Weight of the Earth and the Lightness of the Human Heart   75 coat. He walked on with the certainty that the warriors slept with eyes peeled back and ears awaiting the signal to rise. As he looked darker, beyond reflections of the upper world, he recognised in an unblinking pupil, their deeply resigned waiting.

It seemed to me that the company brought a strange comfort to his journey.

He shouldered the hill there, ignoring the summit with its scattered decoration of teetering boulders, the conical thrust of it from the hot heart below. He found a route through the castellations sculpted by your frosty shatterings. He stretched up, hands numbly gripped on damp rock, clutching on the hanging honey-bells of heather, persuading his right foot onto a high step. And he was ambushed. Not by you my dear, let's not flatter your fading energy, but by his own mind.

He crushed a herb under his palm, close to his face. The smoky scent of bog myrtle caught at a memory, nudged his body out of balance, excavated a huge chasm of breath from him. I pursued his vision – I admit to curiosity in this human mystery. A younger Marion came smiling from a greenhouse into sunshine with a bowl of ripe tomatoes. Her hair fluttered, sweet with the juice of basil leaves she had brushed against. He circled her and the bowl in his arms, inhaling, drawn inevitably close. In mid-stride on this hill, his twenty years of life with her, a barely discernible grain of time, expanded and became (to him, my dear, to him) the heaviest boulder that all us gods could shoulder. The nudge of heat and smell, added to despair and stupor, was all he needed to topple. The rest you know.

Now he's finding his peace with the cold water flowing through the thousand crumbled years of growth recorded in the peat. He sinks towards that rock from which he was chipped, back to where it came from, under the sea. Soon he'll lose his edges, merge back, like glaciers in an ice age. He feels the relief of it no doubt.

He cannot move. Darkness hangs above him, moisture beading on the skin of his face, the face like a map of his past. Put a finger to that line and he could tell you its origin, the history of its formation. He won't tell you now, of course. But he would have done in the smoke-filled bar last night, as he uncoiled himself from his ten-hour drive. And perhaps that was the meaning behind the joke he made with the keeper, when he pointed to the lines of the map. 'Like my face,' he'd said, and the keeper had felt the too-long laugh of the man, like a splinter under his fingernail, for the rest of the day.

Something's happening. This bang. It punctures our still mountain night, though the man barely observes it. He hears the signal that comes a second time. From beneath the bog, he knows it as the rallying call, mistakes it for the Fingalian horn, and awaits the third. Briefly, in the sky he sees the descent of a blurred globe of light. Briefly, it's clear enough to sparkle and then is reabsorbed into the damp thick air, a smudge borne back to the peat. He even hears the hounds. They suggest to him the clink and clank of old armour being shaken down. He imagines it re-settling to the broad silhouettes of men as they rise upright, re-invigorating the gristle in their arms and legs, stretching and shaking, ready for their calling after so many centuries. The recognition of it all would have pulled a nod from him, if he could move. But he is fading from them, exchanging places with them, sinking. What does he care for the fight to which they are called, when he is slipping far away?

Now watch! Unblinking, his eyes take in, but do not grasp, the string of torchlight below. It coils and lengthens on the hillside, blurs through fog, scatters and reforms, fragments of it bitten black by the crags stepping between them. It would draw his eyes to the world below, to the valleys of human life that he deserted some hours before. But his eyes remain blank.

Hounds again, baying.

Deep voices echo, muffled in night drizzle.

Steps resonating in the bog, submerging to thud at the rock.

You can barely see the man now, so insignificant has he become with dark and cold and sorrow. Touch, if you will, his skin so pale and cold. But even with the prods of your bony fingers, he is now beyond the effort of shivering. The bog is closing around him, embalming. A solitary entombment.

Now is the time to gather your creaking strength. Despite the late hour, the grass growing fast beneath you, its sap draining you, he's yours, he's carrion. He's your last act of ice before you hurl down the staff.

You are too slow. Ah, but, my dear, your jealous screech lacks its winter command. It fails to penetrate the skies and peaks. But don't go yet, not on this sour note. Watch, how the torches snake towards him. See how the army, swift of foot, bulky and bearded, spread their light, huge burdens lumping their broad shoulders. Giants. Men of rock. See how they build themselves into a circular fortress, now they have found the body, and their search is over.

The largest kneels beside him, a flash of red in the torchlight. The fallen man, still just a fragment of him clinging inside the body, observes the tickle of something coarse on what used to be his face, and a breath of wind, hot and hoarse and regular. He hears the creak of stiff clothing, and feels warmth leach from something next to him. Strong arms wrap him in the mightiest of hugs, partially lifting him from the sucking bog. And in the deep breath he pulls in, curling with summer warmth, loaded with memory, comes that intoxicating scent.

Follow me. Look. How the memory of Marion whispers at the consciousness of the fallen man, as the bittersweet smell gushes within the survival bag. It is her smell. Her skin so soft. A whoosh of speed and light plummets the man deep back inside the body. A shock kicks with his heart. The sharp pain of his shoulder crashes in, as his heart pulses out to his limbs, to his grazed knees and gashed elbow. He takes deep breaths of Marion, opens his eyes and looks straight into the brow-heavy eyes of the warrior, who smoothes his hand along the man's arm, gives up his warmth to him, tells him he is safe now, quite safe.

Take that chisel now, and look closer, my dear. Come on, be kind for once, you have lost him anyway. Tap gently. You'll discover something between the black strata we saw earlier. A slight rearrangement perhaps, or just a different way of looking. His daughter expects her first child in this slim golden seam. And look here, the quartzite glint of his friend Mike who will take him to walk the Pyrenees next June. Here's the mother, silver-haired and framed, smiling comfort into the flat where his unpacked boxes are still scattered across the floor. In seeking his wilderness, he has stumbled upon an unexpected mine of treasures.

Dawn is promising its dewy light as the torches of the rescue team part and cross, midgies are swatted, a stretcher is constructed, flasks are cracked open, the Alsatian is stroked and rewarded with biscuits.

The body on the hill leans without resistance into the offered embrace.

'Thank you,' he murmurs.

The red warrior cased in Goretex next to him, the man with the cradling arms and thick beard, clamps the man closer to him, turns aside his face, and from the fiery core of his human being launches a 'whoop' of life. It reaches up high into the morning sky, lifted like floating bog-cotton by the dawn's small birds. Hear how it even stumbles the rhythmic breathing of embalmed men.

The heroes of this moment were raised by police from their beds by the alarm at one o'clock. The keeper had found the Volvo with its deeply scratched side still there in the dark, the sandwich box left behind on the passenger seat. Half of the company wait at the bottom of the hill, for news. Now, even without the crackling radio, they know the man is found and alive.

As the sun begins its rise, the mists follow, and so do human hearts. The lower party echo to the sky their own deep cry of joy. It leaps even higher than the first, dancing between the peaks and floating beyond, to the furthest crest of my realm. And feel, my dear, how it reverberates too in the ponderous rock deep below, how the very earth threatens to grunt and rumble and roll over beneath them. Forgive this gravel in my throat. It's nothing. A residue of winter chill.

Dawn is bringing its dewy light, and you my dear are defeated for another season. Until Samhain then, when we shall feel your blue face and white frosted hair near again, the shivered wings of your host of herons. Then you can score new scars onto the hill, and clutch again at human hearts.

Now go!

North of the Law

IAIN MACKINTOSH

An' noo, rain draps drum oan the panes while the skail pipes up a pibroch in the lum. An' still the crone sits transfixed, sooks her teeth, says nuthin'. An' the tundra o' her room is scant comfort tae the man wha bides by. An' the waft o' charity shop lavender hovers growthie-like.

But leuk noo; faint shudders in her faint frame. Clear yer een; her straggy heid shakes gawkily in denial an' an ichor o' drool dribbles roon' the mole oan her chin. Preen yer lugs; her slaverin' voice is wheezin' an' spittin' oot the words: 'Girn an' greet ya mongrel ye! Ye'll droon in rivers o' pish!'

'D'ye no' dae happy endings, ya besom ye?' speirs the man wha bides.

'Nae call fur it son,' says the crone, 'wur a' entrepreneurs noo.'

Ootside in the pourin' freeze, a glaik kicks a squashed can alang the gutter, tonelessly singin' the national anthem. The bidie-by rises obediently an' grudgingly places some soilt moolah in the goldfish bowl provided fur the purpose. As forecasts go, it's lookin' gey dismal . . .

As he waits in the stair entry, gatherin' his resolve fur a drookit assault oan the pub, ony casual observer might just think the bidie-by fanciable. A modern Achilles, he's been steeped in teak-stained creosote an' dried aff tae a beeswax lustre. Perched jauntily oan his napper sits a barnet o' which he can claim part ownership. Shards o' vitreous china huv been expensively cemented intae his maw. The slight curl tae his lip says: 'ye've either goat it or ye huvnae.'

Inside the pub, the natives are workin' hard oan ambience. A voluble congregation is interactin' wi' the fitba' oan the big screen. Hotly debatin' its weekend entertainments is the bikers' club, lookin' unchancie middle-aged. It's hotchin' at the bar; orders are bawled, glasses clink, liquor skiddles an' the laughter is inversely proportional tae wit an' wittins.

Emergin' frae the mardle, a nymphet sashays across the bows o' the enterin' teak heid. She's a fit lass, tippy claes stretched taut ower her curvatures, an' she attracts his dental leer. Then, forgetfully, she brecks the spell by sayin' tae her mate: '. . . an' he wiz wantin' me tae start anither bottle o' vodka an' ah wiz like o my god . . . !'

'Omniscient like? Almichty?' speirs teak heid sardonic like, but keethin' his book-lernin' a' the same.

'Get raffled, ya pervert ye!' screels the maiden.

Further romantic entanglement is forestalled by the welcomin' Eck.

'Hoos yersel big man?' speirs Eck.

'No' bad,' says teak heid.

'Goat yer horoscope then?'

'Aye.'

'Ony guid?'

'Aye, aw right.'

'Ur we still daein' the job then?'

'Aye, wur still daein' it.'

A near miss oan the big screen overdubs the jobseekers. The commentator is rabbitin' oan about little threaded balls. A viewer screams back some obscenity involvin' a cannibal's rosary. The commentator ignores the riposte; possibly the general din, but mair likely it wisnae that funny.

'Whit's the plan then, big man?'

'Meet ye at the fleapit at eight the morn's nicht,' says teak heid.

'That it?'

'Aye, that's it.'

'OK brains,' says Eck.

Teak heid shouders his way forrit tae wet his thrapple. The bikers are revvin' up the machine they brocht ben tae scug the elements. Eck's fingerin' his hooter stud, thinkin' it probably wisnae his roond onyway. Still, that's ane guid thing aboot the booze: stops ye thinkin' ower much.

Intermission

At the appointed hour, the bold boys are shufflin' aroond ootby in the snell wind an' rain. The venue is aboot as appealin' as the weather, but a job's a job, an' they're professionals.

'Whit's the point o' eight when the show startit at seven?' moans Eck.

'Hud yer wheesht!' says teak heid. 'Did ye mind yer balaclava?'

'Naw, ye never telt us.'

'Toom heid!'

'Ah'll go an' fetch it.'

'Dinnae fash, wu'll gaun in onyway.'

So they do. Through the door. It's quicker.

'Twa stalls please,' says teak heid tae the perjink cashier wumman.

'£10 please,' says the wumman.

'£10! Ah could bevvy a' nicht oan that!'

'Weel, ye cannae bevvy here, ya soak ye! Ur yiz in or oot?'

'Wur in.'

'Aw richt. Here's yer tickets.'

Eck is flatly denied popcorn on the way tae the auditorium. Maudlin, he lopes ahint o' teak heid as the latter navigates by the light o' the stars, the usherette huvin' been long since declared extinct. The place reeks o' stale smoke, interspersed with pockets o' stale freshener.

'Plant yer hurdies here!' hisses teak heid. 'Ah want tae stay close tae the exit.'

Eck's scrawny torso hits velvet an' they berth in the chummy seats. At the ither end o' the row, the nymphet is slaisterin' ower the banquet o' a spread-eagled glaik. Eck professes puzzlement.

'Whit's gaun oan?'

'Well, mebbe it's the kiss o' life, but mair like it's hochmagandy,' whispers his partner.

Teak heid tires quickly o' the film, an' noo he's strainin' through the mirk tae establish the audience size. There's some crisp packet rustlin' an' faint snorin' gaen' oan someplace doon tae the left, but it's a fickle business tae see onythin' gleg aboot the rest o' the hoose. He's thinkin': wur late gettin' here; there's naebody else comin' noo; ah'm sweir tae wait fur the interval an' get spied oan; panshit – time fur action!

'Get yer balaclava oan!' he hisses.

'Ah telt ye, ah huvnae goat it!'

'Just look mensefu' then ya gomerel ye, an' naebody'll ken ye!'

Back they go, skirtin' the popcorn stand, headin' for the cashier's booth. Teak heid's got his balaclava oan, tappietourie an' a', an' Eck's got his hand ower his mou, though it's no' plain whither this is fur the purposes o' disguise or tae quell his snirkin'.

Noo they're by the cashier's booth an' the perjink wumman is by hersel', flickin' through a glossy celeb journal tae while away the time. She starts skeerie-like when the hooded yin sticks his neb ben the door, then keckles at the proffered wardrobe.

'Nane o' yer squaikin' – gies the money!'

'Whit money?'

'The till, ya thrawn besom!'

'There's no' much.'

'Just gie me the wampum!'

'Here's yer haul then,' says she, handin' ower £12.

'Eh?' says teak heid. 'Whaur's the rest?'

'There isnae ony rest.' (No' fur the wicked onyway, she's thinkin'.)

'Whit aboot Romeo an' Juliet then?'

'Manager's dochter.'

'Whit aboot the punters doon the front?'

'OAP concessions.'

'Naebody else?'

'Naebody else.'

'Ya gabbit bitch ye!'

'Ya bampot ye! Could ye no' huv goat a decent mask fi' the joke shop, then?'

'Ya gibberin' . . . ya . . .'

But teak heid's run out o' insults, so he just skelps the wumman ower the gebbie an' makes aff sharpish. Eck's no' far ahint, but there's still time fur him tae fire a partin' one-liner in best Bond: 'Yer filum was shite onyway.'

Someplace in the background is the muted sound o' a glaik tonelessly tweetlin' the national anthem.

Intermission

At the polis station, they're watchin' some game show where a flannel merchant wi' a turgid ego is pittin' contestants through their ritual humiliations. Maist o' the onlookers huv hud mair entertainment in A&E oan a Saturday nicht. The phone goes.

'Hullo, polis,' says the crabbit wee desk sergeant, confident nae ootsourcer could mimic that.

'Hullo polis,' says the caller, mimickin' that.

'Spot o' bother at the pictures.'

'Yer audience been abducted by aliens?'

'Naw, but the till's been took an' Thelma's top plate's been broke.'

'We'll be richt doon.'

A small detachment gains merciful release from the tube an' sallies forth. They decide against body armour an' automatic weapons, so they're fairly sharp at the scene. Well, maybe early would be a better word.

A masterful polis unveils the plan: 'Richt, nane o' yiz kin get awa' till yiz huv made statements. Wu'll start wi' the audience since the cashier cannae cluck till her plate's mendit. Let's hae the geriatric party in the heidie's office furst.'

The wrinklies jostle their taigled way inside. There's Chic an' his coven o' three, an' lucky if there's the ane battery workin' amang them.

'Eh?' cries Chic.

'Ah huvnae asked ye onythin' yet,' says the polis.

'Why no'?' says Chic.

'Ah need accurate information,' begins the polis.

'Zat why yer no' askin' me?' continues Chic, fashious like.

'Eh?' says the coven.

'Whit wur yiz a' daen' at the time o' the incident?' speirs the polis.

'Watchin' the filum. Wiznae the bingo, mind. Sookin' a soor ploom,' responds the coven.

'Did yiz see onythin' forbye the filum?'

'Couldnae. Naw, didnae. Widnae. Hudnae ony,' offers the assembly.

'That'll dae,' says the polis, exasperated, 'bring in Pyramus an' Thisbe.'

The polis composes himsel'. He's thinkin': time fur a change o' technique. Nae need fur a guid cop, wickit cop palaver though, ah kin dae a' the pairts masel'. That's whit ah like aboot me, versatile, ken.

'Richt, the lassie furst,' says the polis, smirkin' awa. 'Whit wur yiz daen' at the time o' the incident?'

'Nane o' yer business ya pervert ye!'

'There's penalties fur withholdin' evidence, ye ken?'

'Ah wiznae withholdin' nuthin'.'

'That'll be richt!' says the polis, thinkin' thoughts o' the utmost impurity. 'So, ye were temporarily blindit, like?'

'Ah wiz distractit,' confesses the wanton yin.

'Hoos aboot yer consort then?'

'Scott's Porage Oats,' says the glaik.

'Eh?'

'Sets ye up great in the mornin'.'

'Whit's that goat tae dae wi' the price o' handcuffs?'

'Improved formula,' enthuses the glaik, 'but ye'll spile it wi' ower much salt.'

'Get thae boorachin' ba' heids oot ma sicht!' laments the polis.

Again, the polis composes himsel' an' lays his brains asteep. Ah might jist fancy daen the perjink wifie masel' he thinks, but mebbe it's mair fly tae get a poliswumman an' a'. So he does. Even gets her a chair. Mind you, it's no' the best chair though.

'Richt, bring oan the cashier wumman.' In she waddles.

'Ye'll no' be sae perjink noo then?' ventures the polis, sympathetic like.

'Mmm, spltrr, shloo,' says the cashier.

'Ye want a len' o' ma plate?'

The wumman mewls in fright, wrappin' her arums aroon' her bosom an' shakin' her heid.

'Sorry, clarty me, ah'll jist scrub it up fur ye furst.'

The polis skooshes his duty ration o' Irn Bru intae a gless an' dooks his plate.

'Mmm, spltrr, shloo,' says the polis.

'Hud oan,' says the wumman polis in attendance, 'ah'll speir the questions noo.'

'Mmm, spltrr, shloo,' says the cashier an' the furst polis baith the gither.

'Richt, slap that in yer heid an' wu'll get oan', says the wumman polis tae the cashier.

The wumman squaiks an' trembles, but the ither polis deftly rams the plate home.

'Whae dunnit?'

'Chicken Teaky an' Eck the Sneck!' screels the wumman, then hurls the plate ower the room.

'Weel done hen!' says the polis wi' the workin' gob an' the better manners.

'Mmm, spltrr, shloo,' says the cashier an' the furst polis baith the gither.

Intermission

At the polis station, the crabbit wee desk sergeant is briefin' the troops:

'Yer lookin' fur twa boays. Yin's goat a heid that glows in the gloamin'. The ither's lanky an' his IQ's maist likely less than yer ain. Ye cannae miss them.'

'Huv they goat names sarge?'

'Aye.'

In the pub, teak heid is extollin' the benefits o' free enterprise tae his partner.

'20 per cent return oan capital employed, like.'

'Beats the mercat, big man!'

'Wu've goat tae keep thinkin' bigger a' the whiles though.'

'That's no' the best use o' ma talents, like.'

'Wu've no' made it 'til we can afford tae hire a spin man . . .'

'Aye, PowerPoint presentations at wur AGM an' a' that!'

'That's the gemme Ecky boay, corruption wi' class!'

A biker's gawkin' at the twa eedyits. He's picked up the polis alert frae the safe waveband. He kens a radioactive heid when he sees wan. An' his talkin' machine can send as well as receive . . .

The polis come breengin' through the front an' back doors o' the pub, near enough simultaneous, like. The bold boys have clocked the screechin' an' shoutin' though, an' they're awa through the snug door in the middle. The third way. Liberation, like.

'Doon Bleachers' Close!' commands teak heid.

Eck's taigled. Nuthin' new there, but sumhin's no' richt, an' it gies him a wee gnaw at his vitals. Still, he pits oan a gallop per instructions, shouder tae shouder wi' his mate, a runaway semmit an' drawers.

'Whit the . . . !' says teak heid, drappin' anchor snappit-like.

Ahead o' Cassidy an' the Kid sits a barricade o' scaffolding an' building materials whaur the close used tae be.

'Should huv mindit,' says Eck, 'ah bide oan the far side efter a'.'

'The far side's exactly where ye bide!' says teak heid.

'Ah think the sodjers ur comin',' says Eck.

'Weel, we cannae gaun through, or roond, or back,' says teak heid, 'sae wu'll maun hae tae gaun up.'

'Up?'

'Aye, nosebleed territory!'

So, up the scaffolding they clammer, an' coorie doon ahint some pallets o' masonry.

'Thank god fur the masons,' says teak heid.

'Apron love,' croons Eck, 'is for the very young . . .'

'Keep a calm souch!' hisses his mate.

The polis come traipsin' doon the close in pursuit, narrowly avoidin' a multiple pile-up at the obstruction. A methodical inspection o' escape routes yields a blank.

'Right boays, let's get back tae 'Go' fur mair instructions', says the polis wi' the maist braid.

'Jist a second,' says a lesser braidit species, flashin' his torch alaft. 'Onybody up there?'

'Nae cunt here!' bawls back Eck.

Teak heid jist shakes his napper waesome like, near enough lichthoose frequency.

Intermission

The polis wha does the interviews has reassembled his mou, an' downsized his assistant.

'Yer mate's turned queen's evidence,' says he.

'Ma mate couldnae turn milk,' says teak heid.

'Yer mate's gaunnae walk aff wi' a suspended sentence,' gloats the polis.

'As lang as it's fi' a gibbet.'

'Ah cannae stand comedians.'

'Usually it's the comedians whit dae the standin'.'

'OK, smart erse, wu'll move tae the alfresco session,' says the polis, lookin' manic like.

Behind the polis station sits the polis stables, an' behind the polis stables sits a big metal trough, three quarters full o' an amber liquid, suspiciously redolent o' ammonia. Every once in a while, the contents gurgle an' slop as anither spleut o' cuddy-pish comes roarin' doon the drainpipe. Beside the trough is a wooden contraption, servin' tae lower an' raise a harness tae an' from the general direction o' the effluent.

'Yer honoured,' says the polis, 'Latest technology fi' America. Adapted tae local circumstances, like.'

'Whit diz it dae?' speirs teak heid.

'Gies ye a dook.'

'Kind tae fake tans then izzit?'

'Doot it.'

'OK, ah'm prepared tae confess.'

'Nae need. The machine works it a' oot by itsel'.'

'How come?'

'Weel, if ye droon yer a' richt, an' if ye dinnae, yer no'.'

'It can work oot a' that?'

'Aye, ye cannae whack it. Ye wouldnae get nuthin' this good in some backward country, like.'

'Ah'd get better odds at the bookies.'

'Aye, but ye get mair dooks fur yer money here.'

'OK, ah'm game then. The bath's warmer than the rain.'

As the straps get pit roond him, teak heid's thinkin': this'll no' smell sae guid, but ah'm guilty a' richt, sae ah'll survive nae bother. Must get ma money back aff the auld crone when ah'm done wi' the polis.

As he's pittin' the straps roond teak heid, the polis is thinkin':
that auld crone's been gettin' sharper wi' the horoscopes raicently.
Time ah paid her a visit masel'.

Somewhere behind the cuddy rustlin' is the distant sound of a
glaik tonelessly croonin' the national anthem. Shame he jist kens
the furst verse.

Seaborne

MAX McGILL

She clatterclatters past on a dark bicycle. A terrace of small, low, dragonbacked houses slouch behind her. The street's greyharled expressions scar in the winter gales and rain. The weak sun casts edgeless shadows on the opposite houses. Her destination sits squatly at the end of the row, small darkwindowed.

Pushing through the main door, the light alters. Some squeezes into the hall with her; the rest seems to leak from her skin. It has been noticed before.

The small house's yard leers over the edge of a balding cliff, falling to sea level near the harbour opening. Official estimates give it fifteen years but sandy RIP markers, conveyerbelting over the edge at increasingly tighter intervals, foretell a quicker end. Her father, with time to spare, rotates the vegetables; the most valued get houseside protection. Patches succumb in turn to the inevitable fall, plopping greenly onto corrugated trawlertops. Cabbages found among haddock on landing cause fear in wary Russian crews: what lives in these wild waters?

Displacing along the shadowed hall she calls for her father and meets a weak aspiration of her name, no more powerful than a draught, as answer. Mary is attuned to it, knows he's been smoking when he shouldn't. He knows she knows, and, knowing, she need say nothing. Chopping, boiling, silently consuming, nodding for yes and no, Mother has her own world and few intersections with theirs. Nobody mentions that fact.

It is a quiet house. Mary likes that. She needs silence for her dreams to grow.

Arcing brightly, swelling through the mild rain, the floodlight sheds unhealthy over the fakegrass surface. Energies are exerted, converted, given, taken and redirected until the ball rests at the back of the net, its potential exhausted. Swiftly celebrating, Callum swigs, hipflasking the cheap blend. Heat, pain, satisfaction between lips and guts. A long night, and dangerous to start so early.

Six later, after six, the team's huddled mass swirls across the lino of Clark's, tolerated dumbly by server Roy. Pints aloft, roars higher still, sweatily surging, they crumble to the floor in a hilarious mass, chests aching, breathless with the joy.

'Out! Out!' roars the company, swilling out through clattering saloon doors onto the bluedark cobbling. Even the sky shivers. Slipping to starboard across their bows, old Finlay beaches himself upon a shoepolishblack bollard, oomfing with discomfort. His cap scatters into the roadway, spinning away like a tossed penny. Hooting like containerships they surge on, cresting towards the harbour. Signals trigger memory: the inevitability of the sea. A collective shivering for more than just the cold. Habit and humour could conquer hangover. Let it wait until then.

She strayed from home seldom after darkfall. More, and yet less, than fear. Compelled by interest but duty constrained, she had to feel that she had earned her time. Chores done, rightturning into the street, she took the black bike from rest against the window and, with her right foot, launched herself into town, stretching time imperceptibly on the way. Arriving, it seemed so much earlier than where she'd left. Blends of past and future. Flavours of darkness and light.

The snow crisped beneath her feet, a sound like laughter heard from afar. She had not even seen it fall, earlier in the evening, from her rapunzeltower above the town. Stepping off the bike while still in motion, she ploughed to a stop through a chevron of white. Giggling unheard: guilty at the simple pleasure, a fading ghost of girlhood.

Swivelling her head sidetoside rapidly, she saw she was alone. Pleased, she crunched towards the edge. Ten feet above the inkdark water, pushing balance almost too far, desperately seeking herself in the moonmirrored surface. Clutching the railingtop, stretching just far enough, she remembers not long ago, when she was too small to see or be seen. Now too much notice. And yet still too little. Mounted again, revolutioning along the seafront, she slows-speeds-slows on the crusted paving, feeling the wheels slip and re-engage under her. She's heading towards where the town slides at the sea, as though daring itself to fall off the end of the land. A messy promontory encrusted with jumbled pubs, flats, shops, fishyards. Childstories of imagined risk. Of dark, drunk men percussing doorway to doorway. Outofcontrol brats rampaging. Life, then.

They are teeming now, glory hunters drawn to the players as they surge down Main Street, ever downhill, dragged to sea by invisible tides. Porter's the next stop; tradition required. Callum trapped against Georgie as they try to twoforone through the narrow doorway. Shoving from the team; reluctant pulling from those already inside. Suddenly, they come free, spilling in, turning towards Sam the barman through steamed vision. Overambition is taking Callum. Team captain, morale leader, knight commander of the bar he lines up shots, pints, bottles. All wishes are accommodated. A knave cries 'Champagne!' Callum assents, with raised eyebrow as if to ask 'whosaidthat?', for a second not recognising his own voice. Ceremony attends its production, the dust of neglect brushed from the bottle's broad brow. A respectful hush falls; nervous Sam pops, a glass is thrust under the fountaining gold stream. Gazes fall on Callum: a weight of expectation. He raises the green meltsand to the light, marvelling at the sparkling universe within – 'Champagne!' he delights, and quaffs it in one. His tongue explodes for the second he has to taste, before, backslapped, seized, he is whirled atop arms around the room to the applause of the crowd. Not sure whether for sporting prowess or conspicuous consumption, his addled brain still recognises acclaim. Alcohol-triggered synapses are consumed by desire for grease. Onwards to the Northtown Fry! The charge begins slowly at first. Sideglances tell that urgency of hunger multiplied by coldness of air is eroding fraternal considerations. A break appears in the line, separates from it and bursts into a staggering sprint, a sort of jerky, barely controlled downhill collapse. Hillstuckstreets in this part of town are still steep. The advance guard know that only Mags and Charlie serve this late on a Saturday. For those arriving last, it'll be a longsavouring wait. Oilcrackle; fishglow. Cracked walltiling creaks under the weight of halfasleep lumps as they halfwalk, halfslide along towards service. Good-natured still, Callum is among the second group in, his chest heaving with exertion intakes deep lungfuls of reviving chipshop perfume. Thick with seasoning, a harsh oily pall hangs in the deepfried air. Successful, he leaves into the chiller, now disturbed air. He's alone now, though he isn't aware yet. Intently focused, he destroys fish with fingerends, scrabbling scraps into his mouth. He is being carried down the last decline of the hill, as Main Street blends into Harbourside. His legs run out of power as the slope does, slumping him onto a bench yards from waterside, surrounded by ropes, nets, engines – the paraphernalia of fishing. Automatic hands draw the zipper to his neck. Clear skies now; cold. The crumpled fishpaper rolls from his sleeping hand. Hours of wavebraving toil turned to litter.

This far and no further, she tells herself. Imagining a line on the blanksparkling surface, she dares herself to go on, into the late-night prohibited town. After all, what harm could come? Striding on, rolling the bicycle alongside her, through shadowdark alleys, cobbled ways, service lanes, emerging at last in the open of Harbourside. She gasps at the absolute quiet, always having imagined the harbour as noisy, rough; the boats sleeping peacefully at anchor surprise her. Idling along the harbour wall, stroking the trawlers' forceformed beams, she can sense the longing in them for unbent shape, for rest. Nets curl uneasily over barrels of discoloured plastic. Oil drifts round the boats, painted by the tide into long motherofpearl swirls of accidental industrial beauty. Silence overseeing. Making her way back along the wall, scanning the harbour for anything else of interest, she sees it, lumped on the bench. She stops for barely a second, Father's fears of imagined threat project into her mind. Rocking forward onto her front foot, she tiptoes towards the bench, its paint gleaming dully in the moonlight. She sees a man, alone. One benchbar is broken: he is stretched across the gap, held by air.

Some ancient sense awakens him, slowly, from unruly dreams of colour and collision to the black stillness of the harbour. He jolts, in doing so losing his balance, falling backwards through the bench, hands thrust upwards, childlike pleading for assistance – and finds her fingers. Heaved upright now, he squints, rubs his eyes and scans from ground to sky. His helper is silhouetted against the moon; but her face somehow fully lit, her clothes too clean. Far, far, too white. A girl's face; no, a woman's. Both. Dreaming or awake, he had never seen anything so beautiful. Suddenly awake, sudden shame seizes him. In front of this, he felt like a dirty child.

'Hello, I'm Mary.'

'Callum.'

She repeats the word slowly, chewing the dull syllables as though testing them for truth. He can think of nothing to say. Dumbly, he looks to her, pleading for her to speak.

'You must be very cold?' A benign smile.

'Yes.'

'Here.' She takes off her own scarf, leaning down towards him, looping the thin band behind his ears. She is so close he can feel the warmth of her exposed neck as she twists the thin fabric into a knot at the front. His eyes close involuntarily, inhaling her. His lips guide themselves to the nape of her softglowing neck. She cranes across him, twisting to avoid contact, but his lips close, wetly, gently, on her skin. She trembles with surprise, exhilarated and shocked, pulling away, but slowly.

'Sorry.' Apologetic, confused.

'It's okay, I liked that.' She could feel the cold on her bare neck now; the fading kiss colder still. Unconsciously, though, she has onestepped back from him. He sees the added distance, reading guilt and shame in the air between them. The confusion in his mind returns, the sleepawake distinction fading. Was he still dreaming? What else could it be? Gradually, motor functions failing, vision irising to a close, he slips back under the surface of sleep, drowned in his dreams.

Backtreading, one, two, three steps more, she realises she is alone again. He loses size and definition until, by the time she has regained her bicycle, he resembles no more than a pile of discarded rags. She turns and rides away; no overshoulder glances. Boatchains rattle lightly in disapproval.

To home; to bed; to wakeful, hopeful, dreamful sleep.

Today, outside, the sky torments the land. Tips of wind race along the street, swiping at letterboxes. At sea, things are worse. The nightforetold storm has fallen heavy just offshore. Few boats are out; most roll in the harbour, straining at their leashes: wavelengths narrow, amplitudes increase as the water's rage grows.

Callum, blanched with fatigue with muscles grinding from discomfort, functions slowly, his mind elsewhere. Nagging halfmemories, a dream, a name. His mind toils, unable to resolve a strange notion of light that troubles him. His mouth flexes, seeking the shape of the memory. He finds it: Mary. One word; one outward breath; a sigh.

The wind is whipping now; whitetops of rising waves are seized and cast back into the water. The crew's faces close; no words pass. There is a stain approaching from the horizon: dusk's darkness in morning. The air seems to be as thick with water as the sea, the distinction between them forgotten. Sound is an irrelevance, the cruel white noise fills their ears, making even thought impossible.

A wet fist clutches wood, tearing and grasping through the boat, stretching the tired deadtree beyond resistance, matchsticking the lives of boat and men.

10.04 a.m., Sunday morning, 25 miles off Northtown. Her name but a breathed memory on the seaborne air.

Dr Fenton Dozes in a Shaft of Sunlight that Dusts its Parallels down from a High Window

DOROTHY ALEXANDER

. . . and a texture, a feeling, sweet like honey. I wrote in the ledger. Carefully; I worked carefully, methodically. When I was young I wanted to see death, and when I saw it, it seemed to me the ultimate stilling. Its mystery remained with me always. My leather bag was black. Its silver and glass phials, the hard certainties of its instruments shielded me from impotence; the chemist's labels precise, hypodermics wrapped in chamois, the clean smell of iodine . . . What joins us is outside ourselves . . . I stood in the back row of the choir, my jaw extravagant in its opening. Jubilate. Red velvet cushions, a hard bench, my spine against the backspar. In the attic a wooden box, each side painted a different colour, all bright; four secrets inside. There were many versions of desire, and my body flew to them, longing to make of them more than fragments . . . The body held fast by a long fever. Fear, my lips dry. Scrutiny as a means of description, the moment of seeing, divining; the cure revealed in knots of pain. Fear; a red sky, smoke blowing across water . . . I was distracted by a yellow sun diffusing through a frosted half-pane . . . Palpation, a lascivious form of communication; hungry, searching, the referent pure colour. Sweat, the salt weight of it. A rifle. Even in the heat I felt a personal obligement, my heart in darkness. The mist burned off and we saw deer running . . . The child held by a white paralysis. What really happened? The day's grey; traces of pain, and all the while eating and drinking. Dusk, its softness bittersweet. A blot of Scots Pine dragged across the horizon . . . A change of tension . . . Anna naked in the grass. Something that thickened at the back of the throat and mediated lust. The White Meldon green. The Black Meldon purple. The Meldon burn peat-coloured. We waded in it up to our thighs. We moulded clay from its banks in our hands . . . smooth as silk when we let it . . . when we let it wash away in the river's water. This morning . . . this morning . . . this morning . . . was lemon yellow . . . I listened to the night sea; to waves shushing in loneliness . . . Those who never complained had something impenetrable at their core, as if they did not want to be reached. It was a stance akin to rejection. I felt it as a kind of aggression . . . Mercury when it spilled made tiny spheres and ellipses, liquid, the tiniest spheres . . . We sterilised all the metal things, all the hollow and the glass things . . . I walked over the hills from Selkirk to Cauldshiels. Trees by the lochside bent over the path; their roots made me stumble; the water shallowed into muddy sand . . . There were those who sought attention by being ill. I felt that their neediness had a sexual quality to it . . . that somewhere deep their small tragedies were mirror-imaged in eroticism. How I tired of those . . . Solace in the cleansing of wounds: abrasives, sutures, the fizz of hydrogen peroxide on necrotic skin; pushing and pushing ribbon gauze into a cavity that would never heal, the steel forceps cold, the exposed tissue slippery, the colour of subcutaneous fat and inflammation. Anna, when I held your sweet face in my hands (it was an evening in July; it was raining), cool rainwater running into our mouths when we kissed was exquisite . . . What joins us is inside ourselves . . . The way you gathered our children to you was enough to make the day worthwhile, to make me happy . . . Between the window glass and the dark foliage of the cherry laurel, rain flashed and flicked its violence down . . . Orifices, long rubber tubes, the rubber red-orange that dried and crumbled when it got old . . . The way leaves catch the movement of air and quiver. The way stalks bend down and are swept aside by small gusts . . . What joins us is ourselves . . . Shadow is soft, its edge moves like thick smoke, creeping, silent, moving as the earth moves, terrifying and inevitable. We sat by the trellis. Your favourite rose was pink. Its blooms faded within hours when you cut them and put them in a white clay vase on the kitchen window-sill. I kissed away your disappointment. We shared a meal with two Americans who were distant relatives of my mother. It was not long after the war. They wanted to see 'the whole of Scotland'. We ate smoked fish that your sister sent down by train from Arbroath . . . Meaning was only ever available to us at frequencies which we could not comprehend, the speed of it as awesome as it was wordless . . . I sense the cool impersonality of the shadow's encroachment . . . We found each other as moonlight finds water at nightfall, as silver fuses with glass to form mirrors . . . You watched me shave; jaw thrust out and up. My face revealed line by line. My self displayed in ritual. How the sun gleamed on the bonnet of the Austin Cambridge each summer when we went up north. You declared that heaven existed on the long sand flats of Scarasta. At Rhunahaorine we looked across the sound to Gigha, water and sky one liquid medium that pulsed smooth wavelets, dreamlike, towards us in shades of dove rose and lilac. The sunset reminded you of ribboned . . .

From the North

VIVIEN JONES

The memory, the sensation of choking, overwhelmed him often. It was a snow-fallen February afternoon and he was eleven years old, old enough to say thank you for having me to his friend's mother and set off to walk the three quarters of a mile home while it was still light. She had asked if he was sure he didn't want a lift back. She had looked at the laden sky and said it was getting warmer; it might snow again. But he wanted to walk home on his own. He had a fantasy to play out in the birch wood; a tale of white bears and iced pine trees massed on steep snowy northern hillsides where he would stride, master of all. By the time he reached the path through the wood the first flakes were falling. He watched their slow descent with pleasure, holding his arm out to peer at the large flakes on his red anorak sleeve. He had never seen snowflakes as large before. They were as large as pennies each and would surely settle. Even now they were falling thicker and a sudden wind was throwing them sideways so they stuck to the birch bark. He looked up. The swirling flakes looked grey above him and a sudden gust blew snow into his mouth so he blinked and coughed bending over. He saw his wellingtons were white up to the ankles. A sudden chill made him want to pee but he thought perhaps he had better head for home. It wasn't far now. Over the little hill, across the bridge and up the track through the gorse bushes and straight into his back garden.

The thing was he couldn't quite see the edges of the path anymore. The birches stood mute as his eyes swept over them; they were neither concealing nor revealing anything. 'Mummy.' He whispered into the muffled air which was by now more snow than air. He trudged on, away from his boot-prints towards where he thought the stream was, downwards he told himself, it must be downwards. But, buffeted by the wild air and snow whipping, he couldn't find downwards for sure and now, the path was gone completely. The stinging snow continued to seek his mouth each time he breathed in. He choked and spat. What he remembered with the greatest intensity was the time just before they found him when he had stopped crying, had stopped feeling frightened, and felt only alone. He had squatted against a tree trunk and rubbed a patch of his anorak sleeve until he could see the red in all the white around him. He kept doing this as it got colder and darker until he could only just discern the red.

Then there were the flashlights and shouts and he was seized and shaken and hugged; his mother laughing and crying, their faces all wet, a piggy-back on a neighbour's tartan lumberjack coat (he traced the crossing lines as he rocked back and forward, dizzied by their intricacies), then a deep bath and soup too hot for anything but dipping bread crusts into. His mother had picked up his sodden anorak from the bathroom floor and said thank heavens you chose the red one. It's how we found you. That wind, it must have been from the north.

'Can you tell me why a red jacket, Sir?'

It was pure chance, frivolous impulse and guilt on a seesaw, but he bought the twinkling Santa hat from the stall on the pavement anyway. It would make the children laugh and convince them even more that he just might be who they thought he was. He had overheard them arguing in sibilant whispers as he passed; a little girl raising her voice to insist 'It is! It is!' He would wear it tomorrow on his walk in the wood and if he came across them playing, well then . . .

'This novelty hat in the waste-bin. Is it yours, Sir?'

He had grown plump and was naturally florid in the face. Once his beard had turned white it was something of an inevitability that people in the village would ask him to play Santa at Christmas events; he had even been offered seasonal work at a shopping centre. (His work as curator at the art gallery left him dry of ordinary human exchange though he felt quite intimate with the bustling villagers in his winter Breughels; in fact, he sometimes talked to them in the quiet times at the gallery and felt he could walk in their landscapes, visit their shacks and houses and not get lost.) He would have liked to say yes; to ho-ho-ho his way through November and December surrounded by children, but he declined such invitations sensing that his imagined view of the experience would far surpass its tawdry, sticky reality. He walked in the woods each day, rain or shine, before work in the winter, after work in the summer light. He knew each twitch of the seasons, which tree would come into leaf first, which bushes dangled the most luscious berries in the autumn, where to watch the red squirrels, the kingfisher and the herons at their business. He knew the cavity under old rhododendrons where the village children played and built camps and forts and castles. He was amazed at their capacity to change what they built, to take it apart and rebuild it, adding precious new materials, a fallen bough, a bright plastic farm sack, some ragged garden net. Their squeals of excitement at the completion of some week-long project reminded him of his own playtime fantasies. Though he had a garden shed full of oddments of wood and metal, he never offered them any help, understanding that finding materials was part of their joy. He enjoyed them in silence. He never spoke to them except that once . . .

'And the sack, Sir, what were the contents of the sack?'

The child he knew was Nancy had been at the gallery once with a school party. Twenty-four eight-year-olds with two teachers and several mothers, their high voices like a flock of starlings at dusk, their movements too, criss-crossing the gallery halls in rapid changing directions reminded him of roosting birds. He had shown them the Breughels, encouraging them to look closely, to imagine themselves in the frozen landscape.

'Look at that sky. Threatening more snow. The wind must be from the north.' In response they sent him their images of winter, twenty-four pieces of poster paper with splashes of white paint, some with snowmen, some with snow-balling. He pinned them on the gallery notice-board beside their thank-you letter. Nancy's painting had several figures sledging in the snow down a steep slope. A figure in a red jacket stood watching. At the end of the week when he changed the notice-board, he took Nancy's painting home (he didn't know why but it did have 'Nancy' and a cross kiss in the corner) and pinned it to his kitchen board. He liked it so much that a few days later, he took it to town and had it framed and hung in the living room.

'This picture, Sir, not like the others . . . not a usual work of art.'

The week before Christmas he bought a new jacket. It was not in the pre-Christmas sale; it was much more than he had intended to pay. It was padded, well-stitched with a sturdy zip and deep pockets, and it came down to his knees. It had a ruff of white fur. It was red. When he looked in the mirror it made him laugh. The shop assistant laughed too, then she apologised. She told him the red ones weren't selling because they made customers think of Santa Claus. What about the olive green or the navy blue? Or the red ones would probably be in the post-Christmas sale if he wanted to wait? He bought the red one, remembering his red anorak and Nancy's painting, he felt it was the right decision.

Next day after breakfast he put on his new jacket and looked at himself in the hall mirror. If he unearthed his wellingtons from the garden shed, the twinkling hat would complete the illusion, but he wouldn't wear it just then. He put it in his pocket. Only if he saw the children. He knew school was finished because he had heard them heading for the wood that morning. He had heard their starling voices. He found the wellingtons beside a box of stored apples and after he had washed the boots down, he carefully unpacked six of the sweet pungent Pippins and put them in his treasure sack beside his habitual note- and sketchbooks, pencils and camera.

'Bit of an artist, are we, Sir? Bit of a photographer?'

It was an exceptionally fine morning. December bright and cold, high cloud and the lowest of suns rolling along the horizon, flicking dazzling rays through the tree trunks. He stopped to draw twice; an ancient birch with sharp faceted bark plates and black wispy boughs which he took time over even though his fingertips got cold, and a massive newly fallen beech, crashed through the iron perimeter railings as if they were matchwood, which he sketched rapidly, content with the suggestion of form. From the angle he drew it, it looked like a fallen giant, arms thrown out to break its fall.

'This picture, Sir, in your notebook . . .
would that be a person, a naked person, Sir?'

He could hear the children's voices in the rhododendrons. He pulled out the hat and put it on. Nancy was there with her two brothers and two other older boys. One of them held a bow saw. They were struggling with a mass of holly they had just cut down, pulling it into pieces which they then tied in bunches with salvaged orange and blue binder twine.

'Don't knock the berries off . . . people won't buy holly without berries.' The boy with the bow saw said.

'How much shall we charge?' Nancy stared around the boys. 'Oh, my goodness!' She has seen his red eminence standing on the path and stared with her mouth open. So did the boys. All activity ceased.

'Bugger me . . . it's Santa,' she gasped.

'Don't be daft, Nancy . . . there isn't any S—.' Her older brother kicked her younger brother, who howled and rubbed his injured shin.

Nancy stood up and stared some more. She took in his red coat, his white beard, his black wellingtons and his twinkling hat. Her smile split her face. 'It is Santa, isn't it? Hello, hello . . . bugger me!'

He didn't know what to do. The boys had huddled, the little girl was entranced and he felt suddenly foolish. He reached into his sack for the apples. At this, Nancy's younger brother suddenly ran off through the scrub. The children took the fruit, Nancy first, still beaming, and the others shyly, suspiciously. Nancy chomped through the crisp fruit enthusiastically between smiling at him. He ate an apple too. Relaxing a little, he sat on an upturned crate.

'Where do you live?' Nancy began her interrogation gently.

'In the north. I come from the north,' he mumbled. It was a lie. He came from Carlisle. Well, it was the north of England.

'What's it like . . . are there Eskimos? Are there bears?' She came closer, so he slowly unravelled his childhood fantasy and though the boys stayed mutely distant he knew they were listening too, captured by his land of hills and bears and snowy wastes and his tale of being lost in a snowstorm. Nancy's eyes were almost on stalks. Her apple was finished. 'What else is in your sack, Santa?' she asked. She reached for it greedily, watching him all the while to see if he would object, but he smiled, so she tipped the contents onto the ground. The sketchbook and the notebook, the pencils and the camera lay like imposters, foreign to her notion of who she was talking to. She looked at the small heap and he saw her face change. Disappointment flooded her. 'That's not Santa's sack . . . that's just . . . just . . . ordinary!' she accused. Her older brother suddenly erupted. 'You leave my sister alone . . . you're not Santa! I'll fetch my dad!' He gathered his things quickly and stood up, speechless in the face of the infuriated children and walked off furious with himself. He walked briskly, trying to ward off his sense of utter foolishness and foreboding. He reached home, threw his wellingtons back in the shed and the twinkling hat in the waste-basket where it continued to twinkle. He made tea, which went cold; he reached for a book, which he didn't read; and all the time anticipating the knock on his door, which came at three in the afternoon.

Her parents he supposed, but no, Child Protection they said, showing him their identification. A polite, sleek couple with weary, experienced eyes. He did the talking; she looked. Her eyes scoured the contents of his house for signs of potential corruption. His narrow fixed gaze pierced his suspect. He saw how firmly they presumed he was tainted. He wanted to be friendly, reassuring, but he was suddenly sharply aware that his art books contained male and female nudes, his *objets trouvé*, his woodland treasures, the cones, the weathered logs looked phallic, the novels on his shelves were explicit. She interpreted their significance as she bored through their spines with her detecting eyes. Award-winning filth.

'Has there been a complaint?'

'A concern has been expressed, Sir.'

'Can you be specific?'

'Been in the woods today, Sir?'

And so on . . . their questions piled up round him like choking snowflakes, innocuous individually, slowly burying him in shame for giving the children apples, for liking their laughter, for wanting to talk to them, to draw them, to photograph them . . . Had he? Had he? Is that beard natural? Why the outfit . . . did he plan to pretend he was Santa Claus? That's an expensive jacket, unusual colour for someone your age . . . not very wise, Sir . . . (picking up Nancy's snow scene) . . . like children's art, do you? . . . odd, this is the only one and by that little girl too . . . do you know her? . . . do you want to know her? Is this you in the picture? Is that X a kiss? Just a friendly warning, Sir, no action this time, but probably best if you stay out of the woods while the children are on holiday . . . They left, leaving their spoor to fester.

He was choking again. Standing in front of his bathroom mirror choking on stinging flurries of doubts and defences. Had he bought the red jacket for the purpose of . . . what exactly? How stupid, how very stupid to consider it a sinister act, as though a white-haired man might not own a red jacket for any number of reasons. It reminded him of his childhood, that was all. But it had been more expensive than he meant to pay and there was the hat; he had thought of making the children laugh – that silly hat, the tempting apples, and the intoxicating story and his walk that always took him past their play place. Nonsense, nonsense, he had been walking that path long before any of the children were born, sketching, taking notes . . . he had once come across a pair of early morning lovers in amongst the laurels and he had crept away immediately, not pausing for a moment. What should he do? He took up the razor and shaved a clean stripe into his beard from cheekbone to chin. The wet white hairs fell into the sink, grey brackets against the porcelain. He shook the razor and repeated the stroke on the other side of his face. In an hour it was done. The sink was full of dead beard, old white hairs tarnished grey like old snow. He ran water, sloshed beard, soap and water around until the sink was clean. He looked into a stranger's face, a pink child's complexion not much changed from the pink child of the winter storm who thought himself alone in all the whirling world except for the wind from the north.

Silk Knickers, Hard Floor

CHLOE WOLSEY-OTTAWAY

I blamed the silk knickers; they are bad luck pants. Tired cotton brings less trouble; you don't make momentous decisions in substantial underwear. It is the flimsy, winking lace that creates complications.

It was wet and dark, but I knew a canny route to avoid getting drenched from passing cars. My reflection, acting like a stranger, slipped from pane to puddle, fracturing, receding; never turning to see whether I was following– as if taking so many glassy surfaces to flit between for granted.

Transparent glassiness is one of the illusions this city has recently attempted but I speculate about the collective weight of it, pressing down on the earth. How many millions of tonnes of inarguable living? As an immigrant, I'm too unprocessed to collude with illusions bred from familiarity – there is nothing 'commonplace' about living here; it's an unpredictable frontier, full of reinvention. The cool determination of citizens to erase the final shabby pockets of the past detracts from the urban honesty that thrills me. The blunt truth of my nonentity allows me to breath.

At home, I intended to run a deep, steaming bath, drop in a handful of cloves and light the six stumpy church candles (pilfered in pique, last time God ignored me – then I felt even, not so desperate. No matter how insignificant, I believe in instant retaliations). According to tradition, before my watery ritual began, I'd pull out the phone, without checking for messages. After a long soak, the plan was to eat piping hot pakoras with wrinkled fingers, whilst savouring a balloon glass of spicy red wine. (Half a bottle fits in a balloon glass, which means you feel justified about having only two glasses during an evening in, alone.)

Hurrying because I longed to draw a line under another day, I darted between dirty puddles. Despite nimble sidestepping, my boots would need to dry on the radiator again; the heat is bad for the leather, but this rotting salty slush is worse. Two corners before my lane, the gallery windows were brightly enticing. They must sell more in winter, exuding those reams of hot colour. Throughout December they're open late, offering mulled wine and sweet mince pies to those with time to linger. I smell intoxication every night as I stride by, glancing at the offerings.

That night, one of the windows reveals a painting which halts me in my tracks. Idiotic, I stand in the lashing downpour, stunned by overwhelming recognition: it's a flashback, the thump of an old trauma – I know those exact trees, that exact place. How could this be? She's a witch. Sitting there on bright display, the painting is sabotage assuming angelic innocence . . .

Rain drummed on my tight-skinned umbrella as I stared. Brooding cellos came to mind, the plaintive sighs of hollow ghosts; just as they always had when I'd stood out there, in that recognised place, trying to be tenacious. Trying to respond with resilience. Now, with nature's immensity contained within a frame and a price, I can react coherently. Alive and vibrating, the sky is rendered in thick, oily swirls of black, indigo, ultramarine and purple. Equally alert, the frigid landscape crackles with needled trees and shifting drifts of snow. I want that sky to be menacing, the landscape to give an ominous sense of mortality; but neither is true – the scene sparkles with a magical authority. There is no revulsion.

It is one of those paintings people imagine stepping into; not a generic 'view', but more of a beginning, a possibility. People have leaned to either side, I bet, attempting to glimpse more of that wholesome place, mistakenly imagining that they could identify with all that grandeur. Not me – I've seen enough: those lonely miles cost me sanity.

Slowly commanding closer attention, like the pierce of wisdom locked in a parable, a luminous Aurora Borealis flows across the swirling oiliness; it seems to shimmer, to fold. Even I squint, to decipher if it's liquid animation, or just my eyes deceiving me. It's there; it takes the form of two women dancing, making love – if you care to look at it that way.

I do not have the liberty to see it any other way. Anger drenches me; this is whiplash years after renunciation. It's the view from our porch; everything that grounded her, a recollection of my despair. She's a witch and this is her seeking spell.

Loosely gazing at that painting, the uninitiated could not understand that certain sounds can be heard for miles; like a single piercing cry from an owl in the next valley, or the crack of a branch giving way under too much smothering snow, or the struggle of your own blood pumping. What they might sense is the otherwise pervading silence that hangs over the landscape – a silence that excavates your ears: a heightened lack of sound, gathering beneath heavy layers, rarefied by the crisp air. It was cold, cold; we existed in a monumental, elemental palace of brittle ice. The endless space, the shimmering quality was overwhelming. By then, I longed to be cramped, regimented, to curse congested traffic.

How are you supposed to love in that environment?

She simply said, 'Where better?'

Do abandoned lovers always paint their loss? When it's painted, does loss become a form of truth? Infuriatingly, this was not a recording of loss; this painting was her beloved place, where she flourished.

I was wearing black silk knickers on the day I finally spoke to her. Infatuated, I missed the slinky omen. And later (not much later) she delicately slipped ivory silk down my thighs and dropped the flimsiness onto the dark wooden boards. We had collided. Scrubbed boards like the hull of a ghost ship, or a coffin. I learned to hate touching them with bare feet.

It amused her that I wore frivolous knickers. Correctly, she guessed at the considerable effort involved in obtaining such items, but did not imagine why I insisted on owning six black and six ivory pairs.

'There's a world beyond all this severity; aren't you sick of shrieking winds and lopsided seasons?' I asked, turning to face her. 'Don't you want to see savannah or flamenco or hummingbirds?'

'This is home,' she said, stretching. 'I love it here.'

'Do nomads have a word for home?' I asked lazily; anything to procrastinate getting out of bed.

'Who knows? We came centuries ago and stayed put. We settled and made this our home.'

Didn't I know it.

I'm the nomad. My family stumbled up there (a mere *spitting* distance from the Arctic Circle) in 1904, in a misguided migration, during the short period of thaw: a century later, we were still regarded as 'newcomers'. Back then, my grandparents were determined to turn their backs on the gathering opulence of society; the decadence offended their sense of piety. Inexplicably, they were attracted to the vast emptiness: the breath-taking scenery; the idea of eating frugal food which they personally had grown or trapped appealed. During that first short summer they built their own house and as winter began their roaring fire became the talisman of an ascetic future. For comfort, they had brought a single crate of favourite books and spent the endless nights reading the Bible aloud to their infant children. It had been an exhausting start, but they felt alive, taut.

Like all the idealistic fools who followed, however, they soon discovered that the frozen 'wilds' are vacant for good reason. Their romantic getaway became an all-encompassing nightmare. From pneumonia, their beloved daughter died, because the house was not up to the environment and could not retain heat or fend off the wind. Neither was my family up to the terse communication that allowed for trade, but not friendship.

My lover's grandparents snubbed mine, over the course of fifty stark years; her parents were equally allergic. My oriental mother was 'imported' and never forgave her husband for the cruel trick – silence was her revenge. (From her I inherited cravings for tropical colour and a stark loathing for him.) When I slipped out of my lover's bed, I walked barefoot over the bile-polished boards my family had never been invited across two scant miles to see. For three generations, we had suffered stifling claustrophobia – you feel segregation acutely in such expansive voids. Isolation takes its toll, strips you away; just as solid, supposedly motionless water can gouge a corridor through mountains.

'Tell me your dreams,' she liked to say. She meant last night, not the future. My longings were simple; bustling crowds to knock shoulders against, an indecipherable fortification of noise, and importantly, a small walled garden – a tight order to contain the wildness, a microclimate under my control – nature that I could disregard.

'Scarecrow, shall we go walking?' she never tired of suggesting.

'Where?' I'd ask. (At first she thought I was being funny.)

What about a destination, a purpose? Besides, I disliked being called Scarecrow, even though she insisted it suited me, on account of my thinness; I was suspicious there was more to it than that. For walking, I would change into black silk. Next to my skin it felt delicious; it was fine and yielding. Not woollen or waxed or Goretex. Enticing because it did not belong there, amid inhospitality; silk was part of everything I dreamed of, part of the promise I had made myself.

Supposedly, we spoke the same language; but really, what my lover spoke was barely recognisable. My talk littered the boards like the brittle carcases of butterflies, or moths cauterised by entrancing light. I had tried to learn, just as my father had tried, to ease the isolation of his punctured parents and mute wife. It was no good – you learn language only by immersion. Surrounded by millions of tonnes of frigid water, we suffered drought.

Language, to them, was a weapon used to repel. There's no

special virtue involved in speaking other languages; just as there's no saintliness inherent in getting up at ungodly hours. Antique language should be part of inherited culture; restricted, sacrosanct, a fading aspect of diversity held back from the brink: but they believed their *dialect* bestowed superiority. The way they looked at us, spitting out those ancient words, looking down their noses: as a child, I remember approaching lively gatherings which cut to pin-dropping silence when we walked in. Jokes are too complex in another tongue – we were their joke.

Even with her, my paranoia festered so deeply that simply returning to the hamlet for supplies was an ordeal. What she needed was already packed: wordlessly, the money was taken from me. No one was bothered about what she was doing in the ancestral home, only that she was doing it with a newcomer.

'Salt of the earth' she called them.

Salt is bitter when you get a mouthful. It brings tears rubbed in a wound; you can die of a bellyful. I took up shooting, peppering targets around our cabin with resentment.

'I can hear your mind buzzing,' she said, stroking my hair, intending to soothe. 'There's too much going on in your head; you're exhausted by mental commotion.'

'I'm not the only busy one,' I accused. 'You're exhausting. You're an exhibitionist.'

'Me? But I love solitude – I was practically a hermit, until we got together. Anyway, we live miles from anyone, so who could I possibly show-off to?' she said, genuinely bewildered.

'To yourself, the trees, the chairs, the river, your dogs; you're so full of pleasure, of vibrating life . . . Like a skyful of electricity. Yet you're content to buzz here, alone, in this useless place!'

'But I'm not alone.'

I looked at her.

'There's a difference between people and trees, you know,' I growled in exasperation. 'How can you bear to be young in the middle of oppressive forests and hunched mountains?'

Surely she saw I was a ghost in her house, unable to experience her instinctual delight; unable to accept her encompassing love.

'Don't hold me at arms' length,' she begged.

'I can't love this emptiness. I'm uprooted.'

'But you were born here!'

'Only because my witless father failed to flee the instant my grandparents were abandoned in the bloody permafrost. He should've cremated them – warmed their wretched bones at least once. I'm not feral, like you; I need an enclosure, boundaries to rub against. I'm allergic to grandeur; I hate being buffeted by winds like blades, or getting bludgeoned by this silent eeriness. It makes me shake – I'm unravelling.'

'I want you to stay.'

'I need to breathe.'

That conversation had trudged behind us for months, clamouring. For a year, she erroneously believed that walking could restore my mental health: but there was no sense of the land being *underfoot*; it was not like that – it could not be walked over or inhabited. During summer, it was like the pithy sap of conifers, green and full, thumping with contained vigour; the remaining months made me thin as mist, dribbled by a sickly sun. With the thaw, I haemorrhaged, leaving no more than a slump of damp ash.

During the second year, sinking slowly into the boards, I imagined she would come with me. Of course, she could no more inhabit the salty ferment of a city than sprout wings. Blinking away the intended inaccuracies we survived on, I knew that I had to wrench away. Suspecting that anything started in silk is destined to snag, I departed bare-assed, when she was out with her dogs. There was no note for her to find.

That's how our love affair ended: I describe it as an 'incident' and position it firmly in the past. Over the years, in different flats, I told myself that it was not an act of betrayal, nor a lack of courage; some people are not suited to masochism. Some people require anonymity. In Paris, it was considered *endearing* to attempt to mangle their beautiful language. In Edinburgh, I learned how to take photographs; finally, I could see and love what I looked at: observing without involvement came naturally. The exotic flocked to that compacted city.

Held at bay in front of the painting, I realised that the 'incident' had never faded. Things change, but love isn't given briefly. Typically, what she'd transposed to canvas was the gesture of an exhibitionist; defiant, optimistic and lenient. When had she painted it? Was there a reason for it turning up *here, now*? Why sell the damn thing – did it mean she was with someone else, cheerfully shunting out the past? Was an image-induced jolt a reason for getting back in touch? Regret carries its own claustrophobia. I was wearing tatty cotton pants: a good omen to act upon?

'I can easily turn it around, so you could come inside, out of the rain, madam.'

'Holy shit, you made me jump!'

'Sorry, but do come in – you must be frozen. You've been standing mesmerised for ages.'

I traipsed grime into the gallery, feeling foolish. Clutching complimentary mulled wine, I waited as he lifted the painting out of the window and transferred it to a free-standing easel (reserved for potential purchases). An action completed with a practiced flourish.

'Magnificent, isn't it? I'll give you space to ponder alone. Just call if you need me.'

Gazing at that view whilst physically warm was a new sensation; the air there chilled your teeth through your lips, froze tears to your eyelids.

'I noticed the signature,' I said. 'Unusual . . . not from around here.'

'That's right; the artist is Scandinavian. We're delighted to have an example of her work here: roughly, the title translates as *Dancing Light.* I love the raw power; the energy; and the way she successfully captures the timeless ecstasy of the lovers . . .'

'Successfully captures . . . ?' I asked, looking at the presump-
tuous twit.

Like all gallery owners, he continued to fan me with obsequious
details; omitting the most crucial – her link with Edinburgh.
Oblivious to my connection to her, he rattled on, condescendingly.
Shock made me impatient – made me want to fracture his
(surprisingly) rugged jaw. Why wasn't he out on some ranch,
battling the elements, horse-whipping? I needed to leave.

'Thanks for the drink. I've got to go.'

'Really? I sensed a rapport with the picture . . .' he said,
attempting to stall me.

'A bit too much "raw power" for me, I'm afraid. But tell her I
like it.'

'Who are you?'

'Her,' I smiled, touching the dancing girl.

That was a week ago. These days, silk knickers are only for
walled gardening.

All She Had to Do Was Wait

ALISON FLETT

Her cottage was called Northlands and it was at the northernmost tip of the island but the windows faced east and west. Out the back windows all you could see was the angry trampled grass of the cliff top and then sea, sea, sea, all the way to the sky. Out the front window was a scraggy patch of garden and a cobbledy path that led to a gap in the drystane dyke and then turned into road. The road was dirt and stones to begin with but widened into tarmac as it wound its way past

                    The Fletts

                The Viscontis

       The Ramages

           Jam & Davy's

    The Community
    Centre

   The Post Office   The Kirk
                       and
                       Graveyard

      Holiday lets
            Holiday lets
      Holiday lets
          More Holiday lets
         All
         The
         Way
            Down to the Pier

Mich was standing at the back window of the kitchen, looking out at the sea. Today it was grey and irritable, wee frothy waves niggling across its surface, sometimes jumping up to snap at the saddened heavy sky. She wished the weather would change. A sudden clatter made her turn round. The bairn was sitting on the rag rug in front of the stove. He'd managed to get hold of the poker and was trying to lift it up off the flagstone floor.

'Christ Troy, what're you tryin tae dae, brain yersel?' Mich said, hurrying over to him and wriggling the poker out of his grasp.

'Do!' said the bairn, looking up at her. 'Dadadadadadadadee-deedeedeeedeeeeee!' Mich kissed him on the forehead.

'Sorry babes,' she said. 'Bit grumpy the day.'

She plonked a stack of coloured rings in front of him, then went over to the table by the front window and picked up her mobile. She did

Menu

Phonebook

Search

S

Shawny Mob

Call

and waited while it rang. It sounded like ordinary phone ringing at her end but she knew at Shawny's end it was doing a version of Kylie's 'Slow'. Finally Shawny answered.

'Mich, ya trollop, what yi up to?'

'Och, jist moochin roond the hoose, fed up, hungover. You?'

'Pretty much the same. Wicked Hogmanay party at Jam's last night though, ay? He's some machine! Did you see the size o his hash stash? It wis like a fuckin Mars Bar!'

'Dinny think I wis seein anythin much by the end o the night . . . hang on a minute Shawny.' Mich leapt over to the rug and hoicked a tiny piece of coal out of Troy's mouth. Troy started to greet so she picked him up and settled him on one hip.

'What's up wi the bairn?' asked Shawny.

'Och, he's jist tryin tae eat coal. He's peeved I'll no let him. Anyway, what you up to the night?'

'Bit o first footin I suppose,' said Shawny. 'You comin oot?'

'Whae's open like?'

'Eh, the Millers'll be, they're always open on the first. An the Viscontis. An wee Stevie over the brae.'

'Aye well, yi can forget wee Stevie. I'm no goin anywhere near wee Stevie's hoose. He's a creepy wee elf.'

'He's ma second cousin!'

'He's a creepy wee elf none the less. Yi ken he tried tae stick his hand up ma skirt?'

'Come oan Mich, yi were in the primary.'

'Even worse, child molestin!'

'He wis in the primary himsel, he's a year younger than you!'

'Aye well, he's still a creepy wee elf an I'm no goin near his hoose.'

Shawny sighed. 'Fair doos but what about the rest? You comin tae Tony and Bella's? They're just doon fae you?'

Mich looked out the window and down the road to where she could see the top of the Viscontis' grey slate roof. 'Aye, OK, but I'll have to bring Troy. My Ma had him last night an she'll no go for two in a row. Fancy comin up thi now an we'll get ready thegither?'

'Aye awright,' said Shawny. 'See you in a bit.'

Mich did

End

Menu

* (keypad locked)

and put down the phone. She went to the kitchen cupboard and got out a new bottle of Smirnoff vodka, a litre bottle of Diet Coke with Lemon, and two glasses. She put down the bairn so as she could use two hands to snap open the vodka. She thought she might as well have a drink while she was waiting.

Mich and Shawny sat at the kitchen table with their collective make-up spread between them. Shawny was peering into a round mirror at the top of a wee pole. The mirror swung inside a metal semi-circle so you could flip it over if you wanted to change from normal to magnifying. The bairn was sat at the table in his highchair, streaks of orange baby food striped through his hair and smudged round his mouth. His bowl of food was still on the tray in front of him and he was picking up fistfuls of it and squeezing it through his fingers. Shawny looked up from the mirror.

'What d'yi reckon, Mich?' She had applied a pale fawn eye-shadow base with a smudge of gold across the lid.

'Smart,' said Mich. 'I've got a brown eyeliner if you want.'

'Aye, cheers,' said Shawny. 'Here, is he meant tae have that?' The bairn had a tube of mascara. He'd pulled the brush out and was waving it in the air shouting 'Mamamamamamamamama!' There was a black smear under his nose and across one cheek.

'Oh Christ, Troy!' said Mich, rescuing the mascara from his grubby fist.

'Hey look, he's drawn a wee moustache on,' giggled Shawny.

'Aye, probably goin tae try an get served in the pub later,' said Mich, laughing.

Shawny picked up her glass of vodka. 'Imagine when he is goin tae the pub,' she said. 'How old will we be then?'

'Bloody ancient,' said Mich. 'He'll be embarrassed tae be seen wi me. I'll have wrinkles an everything.'

'D'yi think yi'll still be here?' asked Shawny, putting down her glass and picking up the eyeliner.

'God, I hope not,' said Mich. 'I want tae dae somethin wi ma life.' Shawny flipped the round mirror over to the magnifying side. She bent forward, shut one eye and started to draw a brown line across the lid at the base of the lashes.

'What aboot his Da?' she said, indicating Troy. 'Think yi'll ever see him again?'

Mich shrugged. 'America's a long way away.'

'Did you love him?' asked Shawny. 'Is that how yi called Troy after him?'

Mich looked across the guddle of her tiny kitchen, across the baby toys spattered over the floor, the dirty dishes stacked high in the sink, across to the back window and the vast stretch of grey sea beyond.

'Maybe,' she said.

She could still remember when she first saw him getting off the boat at the pier. It was like a sudden break in the clouds. His skin the colour of honey, floppy blond hair, and eyes so, so blue. Not the flat dull North Sea blue of her own, but amazing glorious technicolour blue, Hollywood blue, Atlantic blue. He looked warm and sunny and she desperately wanted to touch him, to be held by him, feel his warmth seep into the bones of her. One day he'd come back. And this time when he left, he would take her with him back to America and everything would be different. All she had to do was wait.

Mich picked up her vodka and downed it quickly.

'I guess we'd better get going soon,' she said, unscrewing the top of the vodka bottle and refilling her glass.

The road was beginning to ice and Mich had to hang on to Shawny, feart she might slip with Troy in the back pack. The wind snapped at her ankles and tugged at her coat, pulling her this way and that. She was glad when they reached Tony and Bella's front door. She turned the big iron doorknob and went in.

Sandy Innes and Peter Ramage were stood in the lobby blethering. Mich and Shawny shook hands and kissed them both Happy New Year. Mich could feel the tiny impressions of their bristles on her cheek as she went through the back to the kitchen. The kitchen was stiflingly hot and Mich could see a big pot of broth bubbling and steaming on the stove. There were about six folk sat at the table and three or four more standing around it. Bella bustled over to them.

'Happy New Year girls,' she said, and keeked into the back pack. 'And how's ma favourite boy? Come on, let's get you out of there and you can come an say Happy New Year to everyone.' She helped Mich off with the back pack and then wheeched out the bairn and held him dangling above her. 'Look at you!' she said. 'Just look at you!'

She turned to Mich. 'Some size he's gettin, ay?'

'Aye,' said Mich. Folk were always telling her how big Troy was getting but he always looked the same to her, since she saw him every day.

'Would you girls like some soup?' asked Bella. 'Or can I get yous a drink? There's home brew or there's whisky, vodka, whatever yi like.'

'Voddy an coke please, Bella,' said Mich.

'Me and all,' said Shawny. 'Cheers Bella.'

Bella moved off to get the drinks and Shawny turned to speak to Jam and Davy who were stood near the doorway. Mich felt suddenly exposed, standing there amongst all these folk. She made her way over to the table and sat down in the empty seat next to Tony. Tony was holding a silver tankard in both hands on his knee, staring into it. He straightened up as Mich sat next to him and grinned happily at a point somewhere to the left of her face.

'Happy New Year Mich,' he said, clapping a hand heavily down on her shoulder.

'Happy New Year Tony,' she replied and bent to kiss him on the cheek.

He swayed slightly at the impact of her lips. 'Help yourself,' he said, indicating the kitchen table on which there was:

	bowl of		bowl of	bannocks	plate of
oatcakes	Maltesers	plate of	olives	& cheese	assorted
&		ham			biscuits
cheese	bowl of	sandwiches	plate of	more	
	crisps		black bun	crisps	more
					sandwiches

Mich shook her head, feeling something dark lodge itself in her throat. Tony was smiling down at the tankard of home brew again. He was still swaying gently, as if to comfort a baby. Bella appeared between them and leaned in, one hand on Tony's shoulder, to place a glass of vodka and coke on the table.

'There you go dear,' she said to Mich. Tony beamed up at her and she raised her eyebrows and went off again.

'Tony,' said Mich. 'You ever been to Italy?'

Tony turned slowly round. He seemed surprised to see her there.

'Oh aye,' he said, nodding enthusiastically. 'When I wis wee ma Da liked tae go back an visit ma Granny, when she wis still alive. We went a couple times. An me an Bella had wir honeymoon there.'

'So what's it like?' asked Mich.

'Aw it's beautiful Mich, beautiful.' Tony put down his glass of ale and leant forward with his elbows on the table, breathing heavily through his nose. 'It's that warm, hardly a breath o wind. An there's olive groves an vinyards.' He waggled his fingers in the air as if to illustrate lush vegetation. 'An oranges. Yi can jist pick oranges off of the trees at the side of the road.'

'So d'yi ever think o emigratin? I mean wouldn't it be great, livin over there?'

Tony sat up suddenly and turned to stare at Mich, his mouth slightly open. He raised his hand up, one finger in the air, as if struck by something momentous, something important that had never occurred to him. Then he belched loudly and dropped his hand back to the table.

'Thought aboot it,' he said. 'Years ago. But it's no that easy. Anyways, it's awright here, isn't it?'

Mich felt suddenly uncomfortably hot. Tony was sitting too close, breathing too loudly, she felt like she couldn't move. She scraped back her chair and stood up.

'Just going to fill my glass,' she said.

She went over to a wee fold-out table crowded to the edges with bottles of different sizes and shapes. She spotted the familiar red top of the vodka bottle and reached in for it. Once her glass was full she turned round to look for Shawny. She'd disappeared with Jam and Davy, probably off outside for a smoke. Mich made her way ben the house to the front room.

More folk had arrived and they were all crammed into the couple of sofas and armchair that were pulled up close to the roaring fire. All these folk. Folk she had kent all her life. Folk who had been here all their lives. 'What have you been doing all that time?' she wanted to ask them as she shook their hands and said 'Happy New Year'. Troy was sitting gurgling on Gertrude from the Post Office's knee and Mich thought suddenly she would just take him and go home. But then what? She'd be sitting in the cottage on her own with the bairn, just waiting for it to be tomorrow. Shawny stuck her head round the door.

'We're off tae the Millers,'' she said. 'You comin?'

It was a long trek to the Millers' place and Troy had started greeting from tiredness and the wind so that Mich had had to get him out of the back pack and bundle him inside her coat to carry him and now he'd fallen asleep. Her back was killing her. As they approached the farm track that led down to the Millers,' it was obvious that something wasn't right. The place was in darkness.

'What's goin on?' said Davy. 'This is the first, is it no?'

'Aw fuck, yi ken what?' said Jam. 'They're away on holiday! I jist minded on the now, they're away to Edinburgh for the New Year.'

'Shit,' said Mich. 'I really need to sit down.'

'We can go to wee Stevie's,' said Davy. 'It's jist doon the road.'

'No way,' said Mich. 'I'm no goin tae wee Stevie's.'

'Och, come on Mich,' said Shawny, 'yi cannae walk all the way back on yir own.'

'I don't know . . .' said Mich.

Shawny laughed and linked arms with Mich. 'Dinnae worry, I'll make sure he doesnae stick his hand up yir skirt!'

Wee Stevie's place was hoaching with folk. The triplets Fergus, Magnus and Thomas were lined along the wall just inside the front door, each clutching a half bottle of Grouse. Mich had to take a swig out of each and give each of them a New Year's kiss before they would let her through. Seeing as she needed both hands for Troy, they had to hold the bottle to her lips and tilt it up for her. Mich felt a vague sense of panic rise and fall inside her each time the bottle was lifted. She struggled past them and into the front room.

Stevie was sitting on the floor with Rab, Fiona and Douglas but he jumped up when he saw Mich.

'Mich! Y'awright? How are yi doin?'

'Fine,' said Mich, turning to look back out the door to the lobby. 'Look, is there somewhere I can put the bairn doon?'

'Aye, sure,' said Stevie. 'Just come ben, I'll show yi.'

He went ahead of Mich through to a wee bedroom off of the lobby. He pushed open a door and a triangle of light from the lobby widened out over a single bed piled high with coats.

'I'll jist shift some o these,' said Stevie, heaving the coats onto the floor.

Mich lay Troy carefully down on the bed, waiting till he was still again before easing herself up to a standing position and starting to remove the back pack.

Stevie waited.

'So Mich,' he said, 'how are yi?'

'I'm fine. I already said.'

'Aye, but no jist the now. In general I'm meaning. I havnae seen yi since . . . well, you know . . . are you copin OK, on yir own wi the bairn an that?'

'We do alright, thanks.'

'You ken if you ever need anything. I mean I ken you're no wanting me hanging aboot or that, but financially, or anything, I'd be happy to help out.'

'I dinnae need any help, OK? I just want tae be left alone.'

'OK. I jist thought . . .'

Stevie was still there. She could hear his breathing behind her.

'Is that him settled doon then,' he said, taking a step closer to the two of them.

'Yes,' said Mich, looking down at Troy. God, he was beautiful. His eyelids paper-thin and delicately veined, like rose petals fluttering in the tiny breeze of his breath.

'He's beautiful,' said Stevie.

'Yes,' said Mich. 'Yes, he is.'

Stevie reached a hand out as if to stroke Troy's hair.

'Don't,' snapped Mich, and Stevie's hand leapt back to his pocket and fumbled there for a minute.

'Sorry,' he said. 'Look, I'd better go.'

He turned towards the door.

'Stevie,' said Mich.

Stevie stopped, turned back. 'Yes?'

'If you ever tell anyone I'll kill you.'

Stevie looked at the floor. 'I ken, Mich, I mean I wouldnae, I understand.'

Mich sat down in the silence that Stevie had left behind. Outside the door there were shrieks of laughter and the growl and splatter of someone puking up. Mich felt the familiar grey blanket of loneliness settling over her and yet she didn't want to be out there, didn't want to be with anyone who was out there. She lay down on the bed beside Troy and thought that she would just stay there until the sun rose, and then she would head off home.

Strange Glitter: A Fairytale

JUDITH LOGAN

This is a story about two girls named Siren and Melissa, and some boys they know, one of whom is named Alex. Alex is delightful and I am sure you would like him if you knew him more intimately.

Siren and Melissa are snow globe girls. They exist because of aesthetics. Or aesthetics exist because of *them*. No-one is certain. Not that anyone has spent a lot of time thinking about this matter. The girls do not bear thinking about terribly well. They sit regardless, serenely, amongst two hundred thousand identical plastic snowflakes, suspended in water, encased in glass. Their eyes look but do not see. These are the eternal watchers. Blue plastic and green plastic. Nylon in two different colours, convincing artificial skin tones, natural above all. They are still *the* watchers. Even if you believe or wish that you are watching them. Their bodies are serene; they are trapped eternally in this glass and water cage.

Pale blue eyes. Vivid emerald eyes. Open in the dark. Two hearts beating, breathing. Veins pulsing. Neurones firing and suddenly the most exquisite clouds of blue sparks race across the black expanse.

One day I dreamt about the daisy-cutters.

Two figures lie side by side in the middle of a vast green lawn. The lawn is well kept but here and there small patches of daisies have managed to establish themselves. Bands of marauding rebel daisies. The two figures are making daisy chains. It is difficult to establish any defining features because the sun is very bright from this angle, they appear as shadows, but figures they are, and they are making chains of daisies. The two mysterious figures do not tear the daisies from the ground. They use a small implement – it must be a silver knife, I can see the sun glinting off it – to slice through the stalks. I can see little patches of daisies dotted all the way to the horizon. The day has only just begun; the chain can grow much longer.

Oh, how I would love to sit in a field, wearing a yellow sun hat and a white sundress, daisy-cutting, joining the other two daisy-cutters. Threading stalks, choosing petals.

He loves me. He loves me not. He loves me.

Outside, birds begin to awake and sing. The sun might rise today. Then again, it might not.

Melissa and Siren meet, predictably, in a psychiatric unit.

We spend a lot of time wrapped in sheets, whispering in the dark, wearing white cotton nightshirts. Melissa's skin looks tan and soft against the white. Mine? Well, as you can guess, my skin makes the cotton look dirty, in need of a wash or some bleach. I twist our legs in the sheets together while she sleeps, so when she wakes up she will laugh and squeal and try to untangle herself. The mornings are the happiest time. Before the world wakes up. In the lovely soft dishwater dawn. Melissa and I stifling our giggles, sneezing at feathers. We were born to be sisters.

I hate to fall asleep alone. I hate to wake up alone. What goes around comes around, I guess.

The Clinic was a laughably cruel misnomer. The Clinic did not treat venereal disease, nor did it have a friendly receptionist and a well signposted exit. The Clinic was in fact the type of mental health facility you read about in cult American novels. It was pristine and white. The nurses (male and female) were blonde, blue-eyed, and incredibly serene. Siren loved to be serene. She loved the way serene sounded so close to her own name. Siren loved her name. She whispered it at night to help her sleep. It was a comforting, secret sound.

The girls sat huddled together on the old, shabby, single bed.

The television rumbled ominously in the background. The window was open on a moonless, starless night and an icy breeze blew around the room. The room was lit eerily from the TV, the girls faces sometimes in darkness, sometimes washed with blue light from the screen. The girls were eating a strawberry cheesecake, straight from the foil dish it had been bought in – the cardboard box lay ripped and crushed on the floor next to the bed – using their fingers to scoop up delicious chunks of biscuit, cold creamy topping and delightfully artificial-tasting strawberries drowned in a red syrupy concoction. Melissa used her index fingertip to paint the scarlet sugar syrup on her lips; watch this, she pouted, closed her eyes and inwardly recited an incantation.

She kissed the air, repeatedly. Siren gasped and laughed in spite of herself as a cloudburst of pink butterflies appeared, fluttered lazily around the room, and escaped through the open window into the night. Melissa murmured, 'I hope they don't freeze.' It was a sight which made Siren rub her eyes, which all of a sudden seemed full of stardust. Tears streamed down her cheeks as she hugged Melissa violently. Thank you, my sister, thank you. Melissa smiled and wiped her mouth.

Melissa is possessed by a controlled and controlling rage.

Melissa woke up. She glanced across at the digital reading on her bedside clock. It flashed comfortingly at 6:25. She grinned in the blue dawn light. Other people needed alarm clocks. She sat up, smoothing out the creases in the bed sheets as she did so and caught sight of herself in the mirrored panels which concealed her immaculately ordered wardrobe. Her blonde hair was straight and smooth and her eyes were wide and bright. She gave her reflection another teeth-filled smile and stood up. Unconsciousness was the eternal enemy, and she saw in the corner of her eye how he flinched and lost his footing upon seeing her impossibly perfect figure emerge from his clutches. She stood up and inspected her toned, flawless body in the mirror. It was time to begin her morning ritual. To wash and dress and apply make-up satisfactorily took an average of 83 minutes (this was not including the time it took her to drag herself away from each of her reflections, in the mirror, in the polished wood which covered the floor, in the glass light-fittings and ornaments, in the frosted glass of the bathroom window. There were so many reflective surfaces. Some mornings, though this was happening less and less frequently she was pleased to admit, the whole schedule would be destroyed as she would become lost in the mirror world, making painstakingly sure the Melissa staring back from the glass was just as perfect as the other Melissa, the one she could touch and feel). She clicked the stopwatch and inhaled, quelling the excitement and panic that rose in her throat, threatening to overpower her. This morning Melissa just winked at her looking-glass self. This morning she was smiling hard; she had a purpose, a mission. She looked forward to the completion.

Walking toward her dressing table, she focuses on a small antique gold jewel-box, from a flea market by a roadside somewhere near the Appalachian Mountains in North Carolina. She opens the box and removes an ornate band of gold. She places the intricate metalwork around the second finger of her left hand and lightly taps the fingers of her other hand against the inch-long glass shard which arcs slightly and gracefully from the centre of the ring. She giggles and leaves the room; everything is looking immaculate.

Melissa parks and exits the car, touching the bodywork delicately to avoid leaving fingerprints. Fingerprints ruin the clean, precise sheen of the car's exterior. She even swerves to avoid puddles when alone in the car, with a passenger or passengers she is more concerned with maintaining an illusion of normality. In other words, she bites her tongue and lets water hit the paintwork, so she can avoid looking like a psycho. With a beatific smile on her face she walks purposefully, yet gracefully (upright posture, with just the slightest hint of sexuality in the way she moves her hips and glances around from under eyelashes, and the lips). In the distance Melissa catches sight of her prey, no, her nemesis, no, her thoughts refuse to allude to such importance on the part of this *thing*. Melissa catches sight of her irritant. Although her heart starts beating faster, Melissa's steps don't miss a beat. Perhaps we need some background information before the show begins.

Some background information concerning Melissa and her rage.

Louisa was. Is. Was the brightest star in the school constellation. Polaris, maybe. As beautiful as Melissa, as intelligent; infinitely sloppier, of course, and terribly unhygienic. Melissa despised Louisa; initially because her name had a superfluous *ah* sound at the end, which, to Melissa, rendered her own name hideously pretentious. Her venomous feelings increased however, when Louisa began dating Melissa's ex-boyfriend, Sebastian. Melissa and Sebastian had appeared quite convincingly as the school's most sickeningly perfect couple. However, Melissa was not interested in speaking to Sebastian, or even looking at him when her audience was removed and when Sebastian realised that Melissa was the least likely girl in the school to let him put any part of his body that had not been boil-washed anywhere near her, he proceeded to terminate their liaison. Melissa coped well with this by scrubbing her entire body with disinfectant and tearing the wings off dead flies she found drowned in the pool.

Sebastian and Louisa had now been going out for three weeks and this fact kept Melissa in a constant state of terror. Usually Melissa was pleased with her levels of perfection in relation to her contemporaries but Louisa threatened to destroy this by maintaining a successful relationship with Sebastian. Clearly, Melissa could not allow this to continue, and her plan had been formulated carefully, and peacefully.

And now, back to the story.

Melissa continues walking towards Louisa, never letting her eyes wander from their focus of attention. Her eyes are bright, playful and sparkling, her smile still beatific and her thoughts concentrated. Louisa is the only thing she sees in the early morning light; the school seems empty, though here are a few students milling about or standing in small groups, murmuring. Louisa seems a vision in white, with the sun behind her, gleaming, bright, the northern star spilling a faint yet penetrating light across the cement. She doesn't smile when she sees Melissa, the corners of her mouth rise and she *sneers*. Melissa stops inches in front of Louisa, and still smiling brings her fingers together to form a fist and punches, precisely and quietly. Melissa's fist fails to connect with Louisa's jaw; instead her hand skims across Louisa's cheekbone and glances off her mouth, now open in shock. 'What the **** is your problem' are the words Melissa believes Louisa is trying to scream (she dislikes swearing and thinks in asterisks when necessary), but the beautiful and intricate piece of metal and glasswork has carried its task out impeccably. Louisa can only gurgle and sob, choking out blood all over her divine white lambs' wool ensemble. Melissa closes her eyes and breathes in deeply through her nose. She exhales through her mouth. When she re-opens her eyes Louisa is lying sobbing and bleeding on the floor, trying desperately to hold her gaping cheek together. Melissa walks to a bench and sits down. Her legs are shaking and she needs a few minutes alone. Drops of blood slide down the gleaming spike and onto the soft skin of her hand, blooming into flowers in the lines of her palm. Melissa licks her palm clean, watching as the bodies drift over to the bleeding girl.

Clouds drift in front of the sun.

An interlude.

A distant lightning storm lights the sky out to sea, in the east. The evening is warm, and Siren can feel the static crackling along her skin. The world is starlit, the moon invisible behind clouds. The Milky Way is spread out above her, gazing back as she watches stars shoot across the sky, and the crickets are singing their beautiful electric night song; singing in their thousands, millions, one cricket for every star. The blades of dried-out grass scratch against her skin, through the light cotton of her shirt The water in midnight pond is silent and still, apart from tiny mysterious splashes which could have come from insects stepping lightly on the surface, or tiny pieces of stardust ending their long, hot journeys in the cool black water. Back to the stars, reflected, the universe sparkling in midnight pond.

The consequences of her actions.

Melissa can hear her mother speaking on the phone. The voice is muffled. Melissa cannot make out any specific words. Her tone is not urgent, her tone is irritated. It is early evening and the beginnings of twilight filter through the half-closed blinds of Melissa's bedroom. The room is covered in bars of eerie grey light and shadows. Melissa concentrates on her breathing. Inhale. Exhale. Inhale. Exhale. She draws the air in delicately through her nostrils, feeling its tender coolness running down her throat and filling her lungs. After a second of stillness she exhales slowly and purposefully, parting her moist full lips slightly to expel the air. It satisfies her to know that her blood is newly oxygenated with every breath she takes. Melissa's mother continues to talk; muffled, irritated.

A few days later Melissa is on her way to the Clinic. Her clothes neatly packed in matching designer luggage. The car is sleek, black and silent, with tinted windows. Melissa notices the driver is silent, though she doesn't try to speak to him. The car doors are all locked. The car sweeps silently along endless miles of road. Melissa counts the miles. Melissa's mother had waved her off, looking the picture of sombre respectability. Melissa could tell she was drunk. Her mother had planted a cold vodka kiss on her cheek and Melissa had shuddered involuntarily. Her mother's nails had dug into her arm as she said goodbye. 'Be a good girl Melissa' her mother had sung. Don't let me down. She had waved until the car was out of sight. Melissa declined to wave back. She had no wish to take part in this ridiculous charade.

Siren is left alone.

Siren lay back on the double bed. The hotel room was bright with artificial light and she screwed her eyes closed. Fireworks burst across the backs of her eyelids for a few minutes until she blew them away. Thoughts were powerful. Power over her thoughts and Siren was mistress. Most took that for granted; this was a fact she understood. But Siren was grateful for her deliverance. It was like standing above a churning boiling ocean, like Neptune with a silver sceptre, ringed in seaweed and perfectly formed barnacles, controlling every swirl and eddy. Every drop of moisture answering to Siren, the queen. Her inner Siren grinned at this image. Alex's fingers flew along the skin of her legs like a dying butterfly. 'My little crack whore princess,' he smiled. Missed opportunities, hundreds of sparkling thoughts muffled by centuries of drugs. Pills in bottles, blister packets, envelopes, tin foil. Siren had seen them all already. I measure out my life in powders and potions. Drink me. Eat me. She swallowed, saliva. Time trickled by. Nothing to choke back now. Alone. In this white hotel room with Alex, her saviour, her love. 'Believe in me,' he had whispered their first time together. Alex, the one true faith. Dying butterflies flapped their wings along the inside of her skull, her skin, her veins. Happy birthday. Happy

Christmas. Happy New Year. The door closed silently. Siren opened her eyes. Alex was gone.

Alex kills Melissa.

Alex draws the silver blade gently along Melissa's throat. 'You are my busy beautiful honey bee,' he whispers to his reflection on the blade of the ivory bone-handled knife, maybe also to Melissa, and to Siren. His whisper is intense, carving through air, walls and time. In a distant, sunless room, Siren's eyes flutter uncontrollably. An embarrassing tic which had plagued her during her pre-institution years. She presses her eyelids gently; inhales, exhales. Panic fills her stomach and throat momentarily, but she quietens it with serene thoughts. The doctors had taught Siren to rule the world inside her head, and this one little trick of Alex's wasn't going to unravel her now. 'Beautiful,' he mouthed again, for no-one to hear but his reflection. Melissa felt his breath caress her cheek. Melissa wasn't frightened and couldn't understand why her legs were trembling. She appreciated the strength that vibrated along Alex's tendons and muscles, appreciated even more the fact that his strength was expertly controlled and precisely distributed. Melissa could appreciate that. She wanted to smile but couldn't, in case Alex noticed. Her teeth smiled beneath her lips which remained maddeningly motionless.

Life goes on.

Siren went to the chalet with the boy. There was a log fire burning in the grate. From old oak sideboards giant church candles cast shadows along the chalet walls, dripping rapidly cooling wax icicles along the ornate wood edging. The boy's face looked hollow. Siren sat down on the sheepskin rug that covered the wide expanse of floor. The boy flicked the television on. *Friday the Thirteenth* was showing. He sat next to Siren, guiding her head to his lap. She fell asleep like this; their skin warmed gently by the flames, the candles licking patterns of light and shadow on their skin. The boy stroking her hair and whispering secrets in a quiet, rhythmic murmur.

In the morning the world was white, covered in snow.

Cross Words

IAN MOORE

'Waverley Commuter Death Mystifies Police.'

I have to admit I did a double-take when I saw the headline. The only reason I had bought *The Scotsman* for a second time was in order to unravel some of the previous day's preposterous crossword clues, and satisfy myself that the anonymous compiler simply had no idea of the correct protocol. After all, I've been doing the *Telegraph* crossword these last forty years, and I should know a thing or two about the subject.

Waverley. I had been at Waverley that very morning. I read the article with interest. It was just a small piece on an inside page. 'Lothian and Borders Police confess they are baffled by the apparent suicide of a wealthy commuter, James Ravelston-Dykes, who died yesterday beneath the wheels of the delayed Fort William sleeper, as it arrived at Edinburgh Waverley station's platform 13. A distressed family spokesman said Mr Ravelston-Dykes had everything to live for and had only last week booked a luxury cruise on the *Queen Mary* for himself and his wife. The police are appealing for witnesses to come forward.'

Of course, back in those days there was no such thing as CCTV, so I don't imagine the authorities had much chance of unravelling what had happened. For my part, I had been killing (so to speak) a couple of hours in the rather smoky and uncomfortable station café, before making my way up to my new lodgings in Cumberland Street. Having arrived in a strange city from the Home Counties, I had thought it prudent to acquaint oneself with the local newspaper, and after a while found myself toying with the cryptic crossword. I was immediately nettled by the compiler's blatant nom-de-plume, George Wye (no doubt in reality a woman, with literary aspirations, and a surname beginning with the letter 'Y'), and I was soon further inflamed by her clue-setting idiosyncrasies. I managed just seven out of twenty-eight, of which three were guesses. Waverley, however, I was certain about. ('Hesitate at line, reaching North British terminus (8).')

Now the word Waverley was one thing – a coincidence, assuredly, to appear in my first ever *Scotsman* crossword, on my first ever visit to Waverley station – but it was the second word that made me start. As Hercule Poirot opined, once is a coincidence, but twice is a connection. And the connection was the word commuter. It was also one of the clues I had solved. ('Worker shreds curt memo (8).') Waverley commuter. And one had died. The crossword – or rather its compiler – had prophesied the event . . . had they not?

Now if I had rushed into the nearest police station, brandishing *The Scotsman*, gibbering on about how 'George Wye' plainly knew something they didn't, I'd have no doubt been taken gently by the arm, eased back out onto the pavement, and pointed in the direction of the nearest tea-room. Another batty old lady who thinks she's Miss Marple.

Naturally, I wondered whether any of the remaining words in the crossword could be linked with the incident. I checked through the solution, but nothing struck me as apposite among those clues I'd been unable to solve. (And, by the way, they were quite absurd in their composition, requiring extraordinary leaps of the imagination to reach the purported answers.)

So I never did report my deductions about the Waverley Commuter. I did, however, begin to take *The Scotsman* alongside my trusty *DT*. I decided to keep a watchful eye on the rather superior George Wye and her soothsaying. I wasn't disappointed.

However, it was a source of some considerable irritation – my hopes having been raised by my initial ingenuity – that there was nothing for a good two months. You might think a potential tragedy lay concealed in every crossword – but not so. Mostly they are populated by obscure words like liminal, ossianic, maniple and nonagon; hardly the material of the murder mystery. (And small wonder that confounded readers find themselves infuriated by the compiler.)

George Wye's efforts appeared just once per week, on days selected seemingly by random. It became a bittersweet moment to turn to the back page and find her epithet: bitter because it signalled many fruitless hours spent (metaphorically sour-faced), as I tried to unravel her twisted terminology; and sweet since it may that very day beget the delectable forbidden nectar of misadventure in the making.

And thus it happened. The second one. I recall it was a bright weekday morning in early May. The weather was fine and a gentle North Sea breeze thick with ozone gave the Edinburgh air its characteristic iodine zing, quite unlike the balmy currents which caressed the Berkshire countryside. I had obtained a key to Queen Street Gardens – a late-budding, semi-unruly oasis of shrubs and lawns set in the formal New Town desert of regular cobbles and perpendicular Georgian architecture. I was sitting alone on a green splintering bench overlooking a small, rather neglected pond.

Butterflies of anticipation fluttered as I unfolded my crisp new *Scotsman*. Aha! . . . George Wye. I took out my fountain pen and for a change made steady progress, sauntering through the first four clues with barely a stumble. Then there was something of a hiatus, and I found myself reluctantly passing along to 22 across before further – but highly significant – success: 'Gallic legumes done poorly for allergic reaction (8).' Poisoned. My heart skipped a beat.

Indeed, I had to take a couple of turns around the gardens before I could settle down and concentrate properly once more. Even then I could hear my pulse, a dull erratic thud in the base of my cranium. Like a long-starved hyena I worried the carcase of the crossword, frustrated by its leathery skin and sinewy skeleton of clues. I longed for a juicy morsel of flesh, but all that came away was indigestible gristle: onager, tepidity, ignoramus and bumble-dom. Spiteful George Wye.

Then – at last – a breakthrough. The penultimate clue, 20 down: 'Badly stunted, but not of mind (7).' An anagram, and dead easy: student. That was it! Student poisoned.

But where? I checked the answers I had solved, but there was no indication of a location. Last time it had been quite explicit. I re-read the unsolved clues (there were eight), to try to glean from their hidden meanings whether any of them concealed a destina-tion. But to no avail. I packed up my belongings and paced again around the gardens deep in thought.

I considered finding a call box and telephoning *The Scotsman*. Perhaps they would furnish me with the missing answers. But, of course, I knew, they wouldn't (not like nowadays, when you can dial a special number and pay). The whole idea was that every crossword contained one or two devilish clues just to make sure fiends like me bought the next day's issue of the paper. In any event, the location may not be mentioned.

I supposed I could make an anonymous call to their news desk. But I might alert them to my hypothesis. And that would risk George Wye finding out. Moreover, I doubted they would take me any more seriously than the police. They likely got a dozen publicity-seeking cranks every day telephoning with improbable stories. And what would they do? Edinburgh's student population must number in the tens of thousands, scattered right across the city. It would probably take days to get a warning to them all. (And little good a warning did for half the cast of Hamlet.) In the end I decided just to wait and see what tomorrow's news held.

The next day I felt rather like a child again, opening one's Christmas presents. Eagerly I rustled my way through a flurry of paper. And I got what I wished for! No less than the main headline on page seven: 'French student arsenic victim'. I smoothed out the broadsheet on my table and read avidly: 'Sophie Vergé, an exchange student at Edinburgh University, is believed to have suffered arsenical poisoning. She collapsed soon after leaving a popular tea-room on the Royal Mile, where she had been meeting with friends. Forensic tests at the establishment have so far drawn a blank. Ms Vergé was rushed to the Edinburgh Royal Infirmary, where she is reported to be in a stable but critical condition. Police investigations continue.'

I sat back, strumming my nails on the hard mahogany table beneath the newsprint. Two incidents, and both within a stone's throw of *The Scotsman*'s headquarters on the North Bridge. I wondered if I could go along and steal a look at her – George Wye – perhaps even follow her. But how does one find a person whose anonymity is promoted by the very establishment? And just how long could I loiter on the street before becoming conspicuous? I began to appreciate that the job of an amateur sleuth was not quite so straightforward as they make out in the books.

Time went by, and I had almost given up on the whole business when the third one came along. It was in August, during the Festival. Eschewing her erstwhile procrastination, George Wye launched straight in with 1 across: 'Stifled, we hear, by East Anglian jurisdiction (10).' Suffocated. (How droll, Ms Wye.) And the intended victim was quickly revealed in the next-but-one clue, 10 across: 'Royal museum bursary for homeless (7).' Vagrant.

I waited eagerly for the rattle of my letter-box the next morning. Curiously, it seemed, there was nothing (nothing reported, that is, when *The Scotsman* arrived). And nothing all week. Despite Edinburgh's superfluity of disorderly drifters and drunkards, it appeared not one had departed to the great cardboard metropolis in the sky.

However, a couple of weeks later, whilst making my usual cursory scan of the obituaries, a byline caught my eye: 'Tin Pan Willy'. (It was just beneath the name of the deceased: Scunner W., Grassmarket.) A short column of text expanded: 'In memory. A much-loved city tramp, well known to residents of the Old Town, who died of presumed heart failure compounded by excessive alcohol intake, peacefully in his sleep at his regular spot on the steps of Fleshmarket Close on 18 August. Willy had been seen earlier in the day, merrily celebrating in *The Jinglin' Geordie*, having received a £20 note from an anonymous benefactor. Cremation . . . blah . . . donations . . . etc.'

Two aspects of this stood out like the steeples on Edinburgh's evening skyline: 18 August was the date of the suffocated vagrant crossword; and Fleshmarket Close ran up behind the bowels of *The Scotsman* printrooms and offices. It had to be! Another one down to George Wye. Heart failure – pah!

I pondered what it would require in terms of a catalogue of coincidences before the authorities would actually sit up and take notice. Indeed, would anybody ever believe that a few chance words in a handful of crosswords were directly related to what could in fact be passed off as accidents or unfortunate, innocent events? There were many times when I reached this conclusion. However, if there were any lingering doubts, then episode number four should have dispelled them. This time, it seemed to me it could hardly have been more convincing.

I won't tire you with any more clues. Suffice to say on this occasion there were three, and their solutions as follows: elevator, haberdashery and throttle. I'm sure you can guess what's coming. That very afternoon – and as reported in the following day's *Scotsman* – an elderly Morningside resident was tragically choked to death in the customer lift in Jenners department store, when her scarf somehow became trapped in the outer doors, while the inner compartment meanwhile set off on its journey from haberdashery to the food hall. Heavens, it could have been me, perish the thought.

Although this one at least made the news, I was astonished that, yet again, among officialdom there was little apparent appetite for suspicion of foul play. I decided it really was somebody's responsibility to rattle a cage or two. Carefully I cut out the Jenners article, along with the printed solution from the previous day's crossword, and posted them to the Chief of Police. I didn't want them to think I was some sort of attention-seeking crank, nor to point the finger directly at George Wye (and thus be liable to libel, so to speak), so I didn't write any enclosures. But if they couldn't draw some conclusions themselves, then they really didn't deserve to catch the obvious culprit.

Much to my chagrin, however, it seemed the police ignored my guidance. Certainly there was no request for further assistance – I mean, I didn't expect a full media story that would have let the cat out of the bag – but perhaps a coded entreaty to me in the personal columns for further counsel. Whatever they did do, however, it didn't put a stop to George Wye and her crosswords – her characteristic signature in the shape of a string of impenetrable clues provided testimony to her continuance as a weekly compiler.

And as a result, sure enough, along came number five. This proved decisive. By now it was mid-December and Edinburgh was all a-bustle with dogged, heavily laden Christmas shoppers. And – my word – was George Wye becoming audacious: imagine the effect upon my nerves when, over a late breakfast of potato scones and golden syrup, I deciphered the following: Scott Monument Noon Plunge. At last, a specific location. Foolish George Wye! Did she think no-one was on her tail? There was little time to lose. And hardly enough to think. I vaguely recollect glancing at my mantle-clock and noting with alarm that it was already heading up towards eleven. But what an opportunity to show those witless detectives.

With hindsight I can't believe I didn't fear for my own safety, but the short timescale and my long obsession possessed me with a fierce energy and determination. But an hour passed all of a blur; it was 11.45 a.m. and I was still only puffing my way across George Street in the direction of The Mound. With about three minutes to spare (although they say the North British clock always runs a couple of minutes fast for the benefit of tardy travellers) I reached the foot of the Scott Monument, doing my best not to look flustered and thus attract attention to myself. Whilst George Wye might not have been expecting a person of my age and demeanour, a scurrying one would surely invite suspicion.

'Nice day for it,' chimed the attendant in the open confessional at the entry door. I made some small-talk, but my mind was elsewhere. I began to ascend the curving stone steps. It was quite dark inside, and claustrophobic. At the first gallery there was not a soul to be found. I thought I heard footsteps somewhere above, though it was hard to tell external sounds from the thump of my heart. So single-mindedly had I pursued my time-pressed goal, that I hadn't remotely planned what I would do when I got there. I paused briefly at the second stage, but it too seemed empty, so I pressed on, gaining arrow-slit glimpses of an ever-diminishing Princes Street below. As I neared the next level all was silent. Slowly I rounded the corner . . . and made an involuntary gasp. There – looking out over the balcony rail barely a couple of paces away stood another woman – much younger than me, perhaps even in her thirties – but quite small and petite. She turned her head. Her face seemed drained of blood. I heard myself say: 'George Wye?' She inclined her head, her expression unchanging. I took a step towards her – she was almost within reach – then I noticed at her side was a striped rope, of the type used by rock-climbers, tied to the stone balustrade. Suddenly she shifted her balance as though to lunge at me. I was quick though, and heaved myself forward with all my strength, pinning her against the railing. As we began to wrestle for superiority I realised she was trying to loop the rope over me with her left hand. I grabbed her wrist and sank in my teeth. I recall her screaming. It was at that moment that two burly uniformed officers darted from behind the pillars on either side and held us fast.

That was all a long time ago. Maybe twenty years or more. I don't imagine I could handle a tussle like that now. But though I'm becoming old and frail, and confined in this home (it reminds me of the place where I used to live near Crowthorne), I'm still in possession of my sanity and am rarely defeated these days by the *Scotsman* crossword. The nice young lady who comes to see me each week says she doesn't begin to understand how I do it. Of course, George Wye still plies her trade. So I'm patiently waiting for my swansong . . . the delicious but unlikely invitation: Carstairs Visitor Strangled.

Slow Train

MARY McINTOSH

It wi wisnae like I meant tae dae her ony ill, but she wis aye girnin. Like when we were waitin for the train. She wheenged and wheenged aboot it bein late.

'For Christ's sake Chrissie,' I said tae her, 'Gie it a rest, the train'll come when it comes.'

I walkit awaa doon the platform a bit, jist tae draw my breath. She cam hurrying ahent me, aff on anither tack.

'Ye never agree I micht be in the richt, aye takkin me doon, never think aboot what ye're daein tae my confidence.'

She lat a tear faa douce-like doon her face. I kent better than tae answer, she'd won agen. Sometimes I thocht aboot different weys o tacklin her, makkin her stop, makkin her see whit she wis daein, had done over the years. Sumtimes I even thocht aboot killin her, but what guid wid that dae? Sumtimes I blamed masel, bein ower fushionless tae speak oot.

Alan and Carrie had baith left, lang syne. There's jist us twa noo, and we're yaised tae ane anither. Maist o the time.

There's no muckle room in thae airline seats on Scotrail so it's jist as weel she demands tae sit by the windae. Canna dae wi bein ower near strange fowk; she says they smell and it gaurs her bowk. That rule applies tae restaurants as weel so we hae tae tak picnics ilka place we gae, and she canna gae tae the supermarket so I dae the weekly shop. She canna thole pubs – they upset her belly – and she canna possibly hae fowk in the hoose. Think what that wid dae tae her nerves. This disnae apply tae dress, furniture or ony expensive shop that she gets in her sichts. They're different, mair in keeping wi her guid taste.

We wis stoppit at Dalmeny when she realised it wis a slow train. The stushie she kickit up, ye could hae heard it in Aiberdeen. There wis nae wey she cuid sit for twa oors in this wee sate, nae wey ataa. I listened, or pretended tae, for a while syne I opened my paper and took masel awaa tae aa the places wi braw names like Venezia, Tonga, Kalgoorlie. The places I wis never likely tae see. And I waited oot the storm o her discontent.

The time we got ower the Forth Brig she had kinda settled doon but I kent she wisnae feenished.

'I could dae wi a wee drink but, och I dinna ken, tea maybe, er no, coffee, aye coffee. Mind nae cream, skimmed milk and one sugar, jist one sugar.'

Forgettin she simply couldnae drink ony coffee that she hadnae made hersel. But the coffee wis ower het, ower strong and in a polystyrene cup. In the end I drank it, she luikin at me aa the while wi her special luik. I cuid feel my fingirs curl roond her neck.

There wis a femily playin wi their dug on the beach at Burntisland.

'D'ye mind the day we took the bairns . . . ?'

She turnt her face awaa frae the windae and widnae luik at me. I settled for my memories, but she poued me back.

'It's guid tae see that coloured fowk hae the same richts as us.'

She said this jist loud enough tae mak shair the young lad sittin opposite heard it. He lookit at her lang and hard but Chrissie wis mair than a match for him. She thrived on 'speakin her mind'. Aa the time smilin and noddin her heid, like ye wid at a dog. He turned back tae his book.

Ither fowk began tae gley at ane anither but naebody wis keen tae luik her in the een.

The lassie sittin aside the coloured lad wis reading *Hello* magazine. That wis enough for Chrissie.

'Young fowk the day, efter aa the money we spend on their education. Then aa they can read is that muck, that is if they can read ataa.'

Fowk roond aboot began tae fidge, slappin doon books and

roostling papers. The lassie kept her heid doon. Chrissie wis triumphant.

'Ye see? Ye only have tae show them up. If they had jobs they widnae be able tae traivel mid-week wid they? Livin aff you and me, that's what they are. Caa themsels students, leears and scroungers, the lot o them.'

Fowk were turnin aboot and I wis aware o glances o sympathy comin my wey. But I wis fou o shame at her goins-on. I sat quait for a meenit, haudin masel in ticht, feared o whit I micht dae gin I lat masel go.

I turned tae gie her laldie. She wis sitting wi her een wide open. Her jaw had drapped doon like she had jist gotten oot the last word and her tongue wis hingin oot the side o her mou. Her skin had a blue tinge tae it. I pit my chowk close tae her mou.

Nae a bit o breath, I couldnae believe it – deid – jist like that. Chrissie, deid wothoot a word o complaint. But that wisnae quite richt wis it? No content wi the trouble she had caused she still wanted attention. The puir wummin wha had deid on the train. And aa the time her bruit of a man readin the paper. I cuid see the headlines, the *Grampian News*, the clean-livin richtlie fowk in the hale o the North o Scotland brandin me a coorse, ill-deedit bruit o a man.

I lookit roon but naebody wis peyin attention, efter aa, aabody had had enough o her.

We were at the Tay aaready.

'Want tae go wi dignity.' That had aye been Chrissie's cry.

I widnae say that deein on a slow train tae Dundee wis exactly dignified, but it wis a fittin end for Chrissie.

I began tae think aboot aathin I wid hae tae dae, aa the forms tae fill in, the undertaker, the biled ham and sausage rolls; it didnae seem worth it. The mair I thocht the mair a waste o money it grew tae be. This on tap o aathing she had cost me ower the years, no tae mention the emotional sufferin o daein the messages for a quarter o a century.

'The next station is Dundee. We are now approaching Dundee. Will those people who are leaving the train please ensure that they take all their baggage with them.'

I lookit roond the cairrage but aabody wis either getting ready tae get aff the train or shiftin aboot, restless, like fowk dae when a train cames intae a station.

I whipped aff her rings and the gowd chain she wore roon her neck and pit her handbag in my rucksack. Syne I closed her een and turned her heid so she wis leanin canny-like agin the gless. I had often dreamed aboot laivin her but no quite like this. I gae her a peck on her chowk jist tae lat her ken I bode her nae ill-will.

I reckoned I had aboot twa oors afore they noticed she wis deid. Time for me tae get a taxi, pick up my passport, empty the bank accoont and get a standby ticket. Jist for starters.

Landing in the North

MARTIN BOTT

Punctually, at five forty-five, the depot doors slide open and Vignatharam drives his blue and white double-decker bus out into the grey and black morning. The usual, morose huddle of passengers awaits him outside.

As they board the bus, Vignatharam opens the side window and takes a deep breath. The scent of yellowing leaves has seeped into the dank, salty autumn mist which hugs the streets. Vignatharam loves the smell, loves the mist, loves the whole city.

It is cool outside and he closes the window before driving on. In his rear-view mirror he can see that the passengers are scattered like sulking children, with empty seats around them to insulate their solitude. The upper deck, he confirms via the periscope, is empty.

Vignatharam switches on his microphone, 'Ladies and gentlemen, this is your pilot speaking. Welcome to Scottish Suburban Shuttle Services, bus number seven. My name is Vignatharam – Vicky for short – and I'm delighted to have you aboard. This morning we'll be travelling at an altitude of about zero feet above ground level. Visibility is poor, but otherwise conditions are excellent: there should be no turbulence at all, and I expect to complete the journey on schedule. Now please sit back and enjoy the trip.'

Vicky accompanies his announcement with a rakish salute to the people in the nearby seats, before returning both hands to the steering wheel to negotiate a roundabout.

In his mirror he can see the passengers looking at one another in confusion or amusement. He hears one of the regulars explaining to a bewildered newcomer: 'That's Vicky for you. He's fae Sree Lanker. He wanted to be a pilot, but his eyesight wasnae good enough, so he says, and he ended up on the buses. He's always on the morning shift – they had to stop giving him nights 'cos the lads from the estate kept beating the shit oot of him. He brought it on himself, mind – provoked them by trying to stop them trashing the bus . . . Cannae keep his mooth shut, the mad bastard. Dinnae think I've seen you before, have I? Christ I hate getting up this early when it's cold and dark like this. Mind you, 'cording to the forecast at least the sun should be oot by the time we knock off.'

Vicky smiles to himself. He likes to hear the hum of conversation behind him: it complements the throb of the bus's engine and makes him feel he is doing his job properly.

The bus fills up as it approaches the city centre. Most of Vicky's passengers are women, cleaners at the banks and shops in the New Town who work before and after opening hours. Some of them were doubtless working until well after midnight and have only been able to snatch a few hours' sleep. It strikes Vicky that not having to work split shifts is another of the many good things about being a bus driver. There are also a few early-starter office workers on the bus, looking slightly uncomfortable in their suits and ties among all the faded anoraks and overalls. They have probably come from the brick-built houses with gardens on the other side of the ring road from the high-rise, concrete estate in which the bus depot is located. Vicky does not begrudge them their nice houses. If there were no rich people in Edinburgh, there would be no jobs for people like himself, he reasons. Anyway, he too sports a tie – a regulation part of the blue and white uniform which he considers rather smart and wears with pride.

The bus is passing Memorial Park when suddenly a bird flies out from the bronzed foliage and, before Vicky can react, collides with his windscreen. He brakes as hastily as he dares, mutters an explanation to his passengers over the intercom, and dismounts with a sick feeling in his stomach. Once, several years ago, he ran over and killed a fox. He still has nightmares about it.

When he picks up the bird it feels small and hot, and its heart is beating at a tremendous rate. He is not sure whether this is a good sign or a bad one. He supposes that small birds' hearts must beat more quickly than those of humans. He remembers the racing pulse of his youngest child when she had the flu recently, and how hot she too felt when he stroked her forehead.

With an apologetic shrug to the passengers he returns to his cab and turns up the heating to make it nice and snug. He takes off his jacket – that's allowed, but the tie must stay on and the top button may never be unbuttoned – and uses it to make a little nest for the bird on the floor. Then, after a moment's thought, he moves it to his lap. The doctor always stressed the importance of keeping his daughter warm, even if she seemed too feverish.

'That's better,' says the bird, as the bus moves off. Vicky is not disconcerted. He often has silent chats with cats and dogs and even with inanimate objects in the course of his work. He enjoys passing the time of day with statues or engaging in little altercations with obstreperous, badly parked cars.

'You're a swallow, aren't you?' he asks. He does not think the rule about not chatting with passengers while the bus is in motion applies when he does not even need to move his lips. And anyway, this bird hardly qualifies as a passenger.

'Idiot,' says the bird disdainfully. 'I'm a Melodious Warbler – by name and by nature. And I'm something of a rarity in this part of the world, so thank your lucky stars you didn't do me a more serious damage.'

'Ah,' says Vicky. 'Sorry about that, but you really didn't give me a chance. Anyway, shouldn't you have migrated to warmer climes by now?'

'Damn right I should,' says the Warbler, evidently vexed. 'I was in England, heading for the Channel, when some idiot sparrow pointed me in the wrong direction. I've spent about a week extracting myself from the Highlands. If I see another bloody conifer I'm going to puke. It's olive trees and mosquitoes I long for.'

Vicky is silent, fascinated by the idea of such a globetrotting lifestyle.

'So if you don't mind, you could just give me a few minutes to warm up and perhaps a few breadcrumbs and then let me get on my way.'

'Mmm,' mumbles Vicky vaguely. He is remembering the little bird his aunt kept in a cage at her house back in Sri Lanka. He always adored its fluting song and has sometimes thought of buying a canary to keep as a pet here in Edinburgh, for old times' sake. 'Would you like to sing for me?' he enquires.

'I've only just regained my senses after you nearly killed me,' says the Warbler haughtily. 'One is not, you must understand, in the frame of mind conducive to one's usual high standards.'

'You don't want to sing?'

'No.'

'Oh well. I don't suppose your voice is as good as a canary's anyway.'

'Huh! First you confuse me with a twittering swallow, and now you compare me to a canary – a mere crooner, whereas I'm a maestro!'

'Really?'

'Most certainly! Oh, very well then.' The Warbler clears its throat, and as it throws back its head to begin the performance, Vicky switches on the intercom.

It is an extraordinary song. As he listens, Vicky himself seems to be soaring high in a blue sky, dancing with the breeze and flirting with the clouds. When the bubbling notes finally ebb and die, there is a round of applause from behind them. Pulling up at St Andrew's Square, Vicky happily announces to his passengers: 'As you can hear, ladies and gentlemen, the patient is well on the way to making a full recovery.' Then he opens the door, and they all disembark to continue their journeys with music in their hearts. Vicky cannot help thinking how much his family would enjoy hearing such a song in the mornings. There would be space for a small cage beside the kitchen window, where the bird would have a nice view over the city. Vicky's family lives on the ninth floor of a tower block.

'Thank you,' he says. 'Everyone really enjoyed that.'

'Don't mention it,' replies the bird. 'Although the acoustics in this squalid little cab of yours hardly did justice to my art.'

Vicky looks around his cab. He is rather fond of it. On cold mornings like this he likes even its smallness. It is cosy, he thinks, not squalid.

'I hate enclosed spaces,' says the Melodious Warbler. 'I couldn't bear being cooped up like this all day.'

Vicky shifts uncomfortably in his seat and tries to change the subject.

'We'll be almost empty now on the way out of town, back to the depot. It's right on the edge of the city.'

'Maybe that would be a good spot for me to take my leave, then,' says the bird.

'I don't think so,' says Vicky. 'It's still chilly. You'd do better to wait a little longer, until the sun comes out.'

'Do you think it's going to come out at all today?' asks the bird, glancing outside at the thick fog.

'Maybe. And if not, you can always stay with my family and me. There's no point in setting out on a journey if you can't even see where you are going.'

The bird looks at Vicky thoughtfully, and mutters something about people with no imagination.

Back at the depot, a fresh batch of passengers boards the bus, and Vicky sets off again in the direction he has just come from.

'So this is what you do for a living, is it?' enquires the bird. 'Just drive round in circles all day?'

'Well, er, I suppose you could put it that way,' says Vicky, a little put out.

'It would drive me round the bend,' says the bird. 'No pun intended.'

'Why? It's a good job, this. I'm always warm and comfortable in here, even when there's snow on the ground outside. Plus, I've got responsibility: lots of people depend on me every single day And it's not as easy as it looks, you know. Most drivers give their passengers a much bumpier ride than I do. The trick is to do everything smoothly and think ahead.'

'Thinking ahead can't be much fun when all you're doing is going round and round the same route: talk about stuck in the groove! No, comfortable is all very well, but I need the freedom of the skies – the knowledge that at any moment I can take off in any direction and not have to explain myself to anyone.'

Vicky finds himself thinking back to his childhood on that far-away island in the Indian Ocean. If somebody had told him back then that he would end up driving an aging bus back and forth through a grey city on another, colder island surrounded by a murky sea nobody ever so much as stuck a toe in, he would never have believed them. As a boy he wanted to be a fighter pilot, to zoom through the azure, tropical firmament doing battle with the forces of evil. Even now he sometimes fantasises that his bus is hurtling through the clouds instead of chugging through the mist, closing on the enemy at twelve o'clock, dead ahead, instead of the shopping centre at 08.34, dead on schedule.

'Don't you sometimes feel like just running away from it all?' asks the Warbler. 'Maybe it's my migratory instinct, but something is telling me very loudly right now to get the hell out of here and head for the horizon!'

Vicky frowns. He suddenly feels in his temples the first stab of the migraine from which he occasionally suffers.

As they approach the next stop he recognises old Mrs Drummond standing there. He stops carefully so that the door is right beside her and waits patiently for her to haul herself aboard and sit down before moving off. As always, she calls her thanks to him. At Christmas last year she gave him a box of shortbread to take home to his children. She envied him his family, she told him: her own children lived in the States.

His migraine seems to have vanished again.

'And what about the risks?' he asks. 'Freedom of the skies may be all very well, but there are hawks and storms and hunters' bullets up there as well!'

The bird produces a not very musical snort. 'All part of the fun,' it says. 'If you always know what's going to happen next, there's not much point in waiting around for it to happen!' Vicky does not agree. Tomorrow will be his daughter's sixth birthday. Vicky's wife is preparing a small party for her and her playgroup friends. Vicky is looking forward to it almost as much as his little girl is. Soon his Christmas bonus will arrive and he will be able to pay off his overdraft once and for all. He also, because of something the supervisor let slip, has a sneaking suspicion that he might be voted Driver of the Year, an honour he has long coveted. The next time they reach the depot, Vicky has a short break. He climbs out of the cab with the bird in his hand. 'You know,' he says, 'I'd be doing you a favour if I kept you here over the winter. My family and I would make you really welcome. You'd have enough to eat and you'd never be in danger.'

'Depends on your definition of danger,' says the bird, squinting into the sun, which has finally broken through the mist. Vicky shrugs.

'Good luck,' he says, opening his hands. 'That way's south!' After his break, he resumes his seat in the cab of the bus. Just before he sets off, a small boy, sitting on the top deck of the bus with his mother, sneezes. 'Bless you!' says Vicky through the intercom, and chuckles to see the youngster's face lighting up in delighted astonishment through the periscope.

AUTHORS' BIOGRAPHIES

John Aberdein is a former herring fisherman, diver and sea kayakist who teaches English in Stromness. Early squibs and stories were published in *The Can-Can, Ken?* (Clocktower, 1996) and *Ahead of its Time* (Jonathan Cape, 1997). He has just completed his first novel, *Messages.*

Dorothy Alexander is from the Scottish Borders. She is a married, forty-something mother of two teenagers, who is currently in the first year of a PhD in Creative Writing at the University of Glasgow. Winner of the last Macallan/*Scotland on Sunday* Short Story Competition, she is about to complete her first novel.

Martin Bott (34) grew up in Queensferry and Edinburgh. After studying German at Glasgow and London he moved to Cadiz. He currently lives with his wife Pilar and son Lucas in Zurich, where he teaches, translates and writes. He recently completed the English translation of V. Zühlsdorff's *Hitler's Exiles* (Continuum, 2004); his desk-drawer project is a collection of connected tales about a Glaswegian bookseller.

Celaen Chapman was born in Birmingham in 1972. She moved to Glasgow when she was 21 and studied Community Education at Strathclyde University. She works in the voluntary sector and lives with her partner and two children. This is her first published work. She is currently writing more short stories.

Linda Cracknell has worked in museums, education and an environmental charity in Devon, Zanzibar, Glasgow and Perth-shire. She has lived in Scotland since 1990. Her short stories have been published in a collection *Life Drawing* (2000); she has also written radio drama and is writing a novel. She is currently writer-in-residence at Brownsbank Cottage, last home of the poet Hugh MacDiarmid.

Paul Cuddihy was born in 1966 and lives in Bishopbriggs with his wife and three children. He's worked in journalism for 14 years, and has been the editor of the *Celtic View* for the past three years. 'Let It Be' is his first published story. He is currently working on his first novel.

Tracey Emerson has lived in Edinburgh since 1995. She has worked as a performer and workshop leader in theatre and community arts for ten years. She is currently writing short stories, developing an idea for a novel and seeking funding for a short film script.

Alison Flett was born in Edinburgh in 1965 and lives in Orkney. She has had poems and short stories published in various anthologies and magazines, and she has performed her work on television and radio. A book of poetry is due out in September 2004 (Thirsty Books). She is currently working on a book of short stories about island life.

Vivien Jones is a mature student at the Crichton Campus, Dumfries (University of Glasgow), currently in her third year of an MA in Creative and Cultural Studies. She uses her spare time to write, particularly short stories and work for theatre performance, which is her first love and ambition.

Judith Logan is 22 and a final-year English Literature student at the University of Glasgow. She is originally from Northern Ireland and now lives in Glasgow's West End. 'Strange Glitter: A Fairytale' is her first story to be published. She is currently finishing a novel and her dissertation.

Max McGill (29) is a writer based in Edinburgh. 'Seaborne' is his first published story. Influences include the novels of Thomas Pynchon and the films of Michael Winner. He is currently working on more stories.

Iain Mackintosh was born in Edinburgh in 1947 and has lived in Perth since 1974. He worked as a systems manager in Perth until 1994, then as a freelancer for ten years, travelling extensively in Europe and the United States. He now works from home and his interests include literature, football, chess and travel. 'North of the Law' is his first short story.

Mary McIntosh is a retired teacher who lives in Kirriemuir. She writes stories and poems mostly in Scots. Her stories have been published in various magazines including *Chapman*, *Lallans* and *Northwords*, and she has had poems published in *New Writing, Scotland 2003*. *The Gless Hoose*, a pamphlet of four stories, is to be published by Kettillonia this year.

Ian Moore grew up in Leicestershire and came to Scotland as an undergraduate in 1977. He studied at St Andrews and Strathclyde universities. In 1990 he set up a marketing and advertising business in Edinburgh, where he now works as creative director (recent clients include Baxters and Highland Spring). He's never had anything published before. As a birdwatcher, climber and fisherman, he's found it impossible to move back south.

Geraldine Perriam is 46 and lives in the country north of Glasgow with her husband, hens and a cat. Publications include poetry, book reviews and articles on fiction. She is currently editing a *Festschrift* celebrating the life and works of the Scottish writer Josephine Tey, to be published in July 2004. Main works in progress include a novel set in Dumfries and Galloway during the foot and mouth crisis, and a novel set in 1930s' Shanghai.

Lydia Robb writes poetry and prose in both English and Scots. She has been published in various anthologies including two Polygon collections, *Shorts*. Recipient of a number of literary prizes, she was awarded a Scottish Arts Council Writers' Bursary in 1998. A collection of poetry, *Last Tango with Magritte*, was published by Chapman in 2001.

Kenneth Shand (24) was born in Aberdeen and lives in Glasgow. He studied Creative Writing at Edinburgh University where he won the Sloane Prize for poetry. Future projects include a collection of short stories, a play about cosmonauts and a novel based on the Darien Scheme.

Rob McClure Smith is an expatriate Scot currently living on the Illinois prairie. He has published his short fiction in a number of American literary magazines. He is currently working on a manuscript about punk rock, soccer and bigotry in Glasgow in the 1970s.

Evelyn Weir was born and brought up in Glasgow, now lives in East Lothian and has one young daughter. Having enjoyed writing poetry since early childhood, Evelyn has also written for magazines and academic journals, and has recently begun to write fiction. Evelyn is presently working on a short story collection.

Chloe Wolsey-Ottaway (31) writes every day, in Edinburgh, stopping only for coffee with friends. Weekends are spent with her partner Heather and their dog, Sasha. In 2003, Chloe's work was published in 'Richard and Judy's Winning Stories'. Currently, Chloe has multiple stories on the go, for folk of all ages.